THREE PASSIONATE WOMEN WITH ONE THING IN COMMON . . .

ROSALIE—Beverly Hills beauty, her rock marriage to a top Hollywood producer had lef her sexually starved, hungry to be in the arms o just one man. . . .

CHRYSTAL—Starry-eyed New Jersey writer she had given birth to one man's child and mar ried another . . . the wrong man. Now she had to make it right. . . .

DAPHNE—Fabulously successful model, hand some men begged to get into her bed, but none could bring her the satisfaction of the one lover she just had to meet again. . . .

WOULD THEY GET THEIR CHANCE T RECAPTURE A DREAM—OR DISCOVER SHOCKING SECRET BEYOND IMAGININC

Also by Susan Lois

PERSONALS

Reunion Affairs

Susan Lois

A DELL BOOK

Published by
Dell Publishing
a division of
The Bantam Doubleday Dell
Publishing Group, Inc.
666 Fifth Avenue
New York, New York 10103

ISBN: 0-440-20213-2

Printed in the United States of America

Published simultaneously in Canada

November 1988

10 9 8 7 6 5 4 3 2 1

OPM

*This book is dedicated to
Allan and Mike*

PART ONE
Coming Apart

CHAPTER ONE

Rosalie

He'd been on top of her for ages but nothing was happening.

"Maybe I should talk dirty to you . . ." she ventured.

Kermit sighed. "What can you say that you haven't already said?"

"Fuck me, stud," Rosalie tried, lowering her voice to a sexy contralto.

"You've already said that," he reminded her. "Say something else."

For a moment her mind went blank. If he'd asked for a critique of Freud's *Moses and Monotheism* or an analysis of Sartre's *Being and Nothingness,* she could deliver. But innovative dirty talk was something else.

She closed her eyes and tightened her legs around him. "I love your big long *thing* inside me," she said.

Kermit lay still. A bump on a log.

This was going to be tougher than she thought. "I love your pookie, your hot rod, your ding-a-ling. . . ."

He rolled off her. "Jesus, Rosalie. I'm fifty-eight years old and you're talking ding-a-ling!"

She cursed silently to herself. Why couldn't the winner of the Emily Dickinson Award for Creative Use of English come up with a better fuck phrase?

For long moments they lay silent, not touching. Then he patted her arm. "Don't worry about it," he said condescendingly. "Maybe next time."

Again next time? How many "next times" had there been in the last six months? Rosalie wondered. She was afraid to count. Next to her, Kermit feigned a yawn.

"Well," he said, "I gotta hustle. I should have been at the studio an hour ago." He made a dash for the bathroom.

Seconds later Rosalie heard the shower going full blast. She sighed and pulled the sheet to her chin. Satin sheets. She had actually resorted to satin sheets. Two hundred and fifty dollars for the fitted bottom, two-twenty-five for the top sheet. And he hadn't even noticed.

She was close to tears. This impotency business—if that's what it really was—was getting serious. Her best friend, Angelica, had been through it with her husband, Franklin. "It was the downers that did it," Angelica had confided. "When they take downers they never can get it up."

But as far as she knew, Kermit, unlike most people in the business, wasn't on downers. Or uppers either, for that matter. So what was his problem?

Maybe *she* was his problem.

It wasn't as though she hadn't tried. A month ago she'd driven over to that sleazy little shop on Santa Monica Boulevard and bought one of those Ultra-Allure push-up bras and matching crotchless panties. The smirking transvestite behind the counter claimed no man could resist such enticements.

Well, she knew one man who could.

Kermit had taken one look and made a face. "You look like a *nafka* in that getup!" he'd proclaimed. "A regular whoo-er!" Seeing the hurt in her face, he'd hastily amended, "No offense intended, Rosalie."

When the "getup" didn't work she'd tried Spurt—a $300-an-ounce scent concocted by Bruce of Beverly Hills that allegedly contained aphrodisiacal powers. "Darling," Bruce had gushed, "this little blend comes directly from the leaf of the fornica tree, which is indigenous to the banks of the Amazon River. And you know what they say about those Amazons. . . ." Bruce winked lasciviously.

From the expression on Bruce's face, she got the general idea. "The Formica tree, huh?"

Bruce rolled his eyes. "Not Formica!" he screamed. *"Fornica! Fornica!* You know," he said, making a circle of his thumb and forefinger and obscenely poking his other finger through it.

Rosalie blushed. Three hundred dollars an ounce was a hell of a lot to spend on nectar from a tree she'd never even heard of, but she was desperate. What did she have to lose, anyway?

Only a night's sleep, as it turned out. Kermit, always allergy-prone, took one whiff of Spurt and erupted into a nightlong fit of sneezing. Finally, at dawn, he took his pillow and moved to the guest room down the hall.

That's when Sedilla came into the act. Haggard and bleary-eyed, Rosalie had stumbled from their bedroom into the kitchen, where Sedilla had already prepared the coffee. Sweet, efficient Sedilla had been with them forever, it seemed. Now she looked at Rosalie and clucked sympathetically.

"You no sleep so good, *si?* The sneezy, huh?"

"Si," Rosalie sighed. "Señor Fineberg had a rough night."

Sedilla smoothed her apron over her ample torso and sat down across the table from Rosalie. She looked around carefully to make sure they were alone. Even from here they heard the buzzlike sounds of Kermit's snores from the guest room above them.

"I have som'tin' for you, Meesus Eff," Sedilla said conspiratorially. From the pocket of her apron she produced a small glassene envelope and slid it across the table to Rosalie.

Rosalie stared at the envelope. Cocaine? she wondered. Smack? Powdered sugar? "What *is* this, Sedilla?" she asked suspiciously.

Sedilla smiled and nodded. "Ees good stoff, Meesus Eff."

Rosalie frowned.

Sedilla reached over and patted her arm. "Take eet," she urged gently. "Ees for your hospond . . ." She paused and looked around once again. "Ees make it go *op,*" she whispered. "De pecker," she explained.

Rosalie blinked. How did Sedilla know? Was it that obvious? Obviously it was. She looked at Sedilla. A glimmer of womanly camaraderie passed between them.

Sedilla pointed to the envelope. "Ees ancient Aztec remedy for no-fuckee," she explained. "Everybody need sometime. . . ."

Without another word Rosalie pocketed the envelope. Aztecs, Amazons . . . she'd try anything to get Kermit functioning again.

That evening at dinner she discreetly slipped the Aztec potion into Kermit's wine. She held her glass up high and proposed a toast. "To us," she said with an encouraging smile.

Kermit threw her a quizzical glance and took a sip. He grimaced and spat it out.

"Good god, Rosalie! What the hell kinda wine is this?"

Rosalie tried her best to look innocent. "It's that Vouvray that Nicholson gave us last year. Remember? You told me to order a case of it?"

"I did?" Kermit said. "Well, it tastes like Montezuma's revenge! Yuck!"

Rosalie watched him get up and go to the liquor cabinet and pour himself a glass of port. Silently, she shrugged. Well, he was close. Montezuma was an Aztec.

So here she was, thirty-eight years old, fresh out of alternatives.

So what *was* it with Kermit?

Until about six months ago he'd depended on her implicitly. For years she'd been his script consultant, advising him on every detail of every project that crossed his desk. For nearly seventeen years of marriage she had been his Rosalyn Carter, his Nancy Reagan, his Leona Helmsley. The power behind his moviedom throne.

"You're the smartest cookie I ever met, Rosalie," he used to say. But now the cookie seemed to be crumbling.

He hadn't said word one to her about his new picture, *Yesterday's News*. She'd had to hear about it from Angelica. And then she'd seen the ad in *Variety:*

Kermit O. Fineberg
in association with
Elizabeth Barclay
presents
YESTERDAY'S NEWS
The Romantic Thriller/Comedy/Drama
of the Ages!

Rosalie had read the ad once, twice, and then she read it again. *Who the hell was Elizabeth Barclay?*

She asked him.

"Just an old maid shiksa with big bucks," he told her. "She was a script girl for Huston, remember?"

Rosalie didn't remember, but she didn't pursue it. Something told her not to.

But maybe it was time.

Now Kermit reentered their bedroom with a towel wrapped around his burgeoning middle. She saw him glance at her and quickly look away.

"Kermit," she began. "We have to talk."

"Nothing like a hot shower to get the blood moving again," he said.

She gave him a withering look. "Kermit, I mean it. We have to talk."

"Sure," he said, placatingly. "Tonight." He

moved quickly to his closet and studied the contents.

"Not tonight. *Now,*" she insisted. When he remained silent she swallowed and asked, "Kermit, does our problem have anything to do with Elizabeth Barclay?"

He didn't flinch. He held up a white silk shirt from Lew Magram. "What do you think, Rosalie?"

"Kermit, you're not listening. I want to know—"

He cut her off. "For God's sake, Rosalie!" he burst out angrily. "Once or twice I can't get it up and you make a whole megillah!"

Should she remind him that "once or twice" was really six months? She decided to say nothing for the moment.

"Listen, Rosalie," he said, hastily pulling on his underwear. "I don't wanna fight. I got enough trouble at the studio. . . ."

But she barely heard him. She couldn't believe what she was seeing: *red silk bikini briefs!* Her Kermit, who'd always favored cotton boxer shorts, was now into red silk undies with golden fleurs-de-lis!

He kept rattling on. Inconsequential details of production. Lighting problems. Director troubles. Costuming glitches.

"To tell you the truth, Rosalie, I made a mistake. I was embarrassed to say anything. I'm in too deep now and I can't see a way out. Even

Coppola didn't have such *tsouris* in his darkest hours. . . ."

But why the red silk underwear?

She watched him zip his new Armani trousers. They fit him like a second skin. He slipped another gold chain around his neck, stepped casually into his snakeskin Gucci loafers, and took a final look in the mirror.

She watched him watching himself. Somehow Kermit didn't look like a defeated man. Rather, he looked like a man who was definitely up to something.

But what? And with whom?

She didn't feel like getting out of bed. On the other hand, she didn't feel like staying *in* bed, either. Better to get busy. Slowly she put one foot on the floor and then the other and pushed herself up. What was she going to do about Kermit? And about Josie?

Josie'd stayed home from school again this morning, complaining of a stomachache. The second time in two weeks! Josie, who'd never missed a day of school until this year.

Rosalie padded through the mirrored dressing room. Seven Rosalies stared back at her. Seven dark-eyed, not-quite-beautiful redheads. She forced herself to take inventory. The skin was clear. The teeth were even and white, the grin slightly crooked. The hips were still slender and finely shaped; the breasts were still full and high; the flat stomach gave no indication that she was the mother of a teenager.

Again the thought of Josie troubled her. The kid had had a perfect score on the SAT's, but that was before the rhinoplasty. . . .

Rosalie shook the worrisome thoughts away and willed herself to get on with the appraisal. Molded thighs as good as any shiksa's. As good as old Elizabeth Barclay's, she would bet. She turned and looked over her shoulder. An ass she could be proud of. Kermit was an ass man, Rosalie knew. Maybe that was one reason why he'd married her. Not the only reason of course. He *had* loved her. She was sure of it. And she had loved him enough. After all, he had saved her from the shame of being an unwed mother all those years ago, when unwed mothers were still the pariahs of society.

Seventeen years of marriage to Kermit. Seventeen years since Bloom . . .

At the thought of Bloom she could see her features softening, becoming prettier. Not that she had ever been beautiful. What was it her mother used to say? "Rosalie, darling, you know I love you, but the truth is the truth. Your face will never be your fortune. You'll have to use your brains to get anywhere in this world."

Still, when she and Bloom had been lovers, she'd been as close to beautiful as she would ever be. . . .

* * *

"My beautiful, my perfect rose," he'd said,
sliding his hand between her thighs. The light in
the cave glowed iridescently upon them. "So
soft, so delicate, so incredibly beautiful," he
crooned as his fingers parted the lips of her secret place.

"I'll love you forever," she whispered as she
gave herself totally to him.

"My rose," he said.

She was his rose. She would always be his rose.
She opened the mirrored closet door and
reached up. The tin of potpourri slipped easily
into her hands. How clever she was to have
taken that potpourri preparation and flower-
drying class at the L.A. Botanical Garden when
she'd decided to save Bloom's birthday roses.
Every year they came. He hadn't forgotten her.
She smiled. Like Josie, the roses were her link to
the man she had loved so completely.

She pried open the lid and sniffed. Instantly
she was transported across miles and time to
Windsor College. The best four years of her life.
She felt the familiar thrill even after all this
time. She, Rosalie Samotsky Fineberg, was and
always would be a Windsor girl.

She could still hear her father and mother
arguing in the little kitchen of the Bakersfield
house as, upstairs, in her cubbyhole of a bed-

room, she packed her trunk for her first year there.

"Better we should send her to typing school!" her father had screamed.

"Greenhorn!" her mother had shrieked back. "Ignorant peasant! This is America, the golden land, where a Jewish girl can grow up to be anything she wants to be! Look at Bess Meyerson!"

"Bess Meyerson is a beautiful girl!" her father pointed out. "Our Rosalie ain't so beautiful. . . ."

"Maybe so, Jake. Maybe so. But Rosalie's got brains. Why you think she got a scholarship?"

But scholarship or no, Rosalie had made up her mind to go to Windsor. It was a good school, sure. But that wasn't the only reason. She'd selected Windsor College because that was where Josiah Mendelsohn Bloom taught. By the time she'd graduated from high school she'd already read every book he'd ever written at least twice. Rosalie Samotsky was already a little in love with Bloom before she ever met him.

Now she heard Sedilla bustling about in the hallway. Reluctantly, she replaced the potpourri tin on the closet shelf and stepped into the shower.

It was best not to dwell on the past, she told herself.

* * *

But the past was not to be denied.

It intruded into the present via the noon mail.

Dressed in designer denim, her flaming red
hair held back by an expensive tortoise-shell
comb, Josie scooped up the mail before Sedilla
could get to it. Impatiently, she riffled through it
and then, with a sigh, tossed it at Rosalie. "I'm
going out," she said, slipping on the Gianfranco
Grambella sunglasses from Giorgio.

Rosalie looked up. There was so much she
wanted to say to Josie. She wanted to take her
daughter into her arms and give her a big hug
and tell her everything was going to be all right.
But of course she didn't. "Will you be back
soon?"

Josie shrugged. "Who knows?"

Rosalie heard Sedilla switch on the vacuum
cleaner in the living room. No chance of reaching Josie now. Still, she would have given anything to know what was troubling her daughter.
It had been two months since Josie's nose job,
and all traces of the operation had vanished.
Josie was beautiful now, but she was a different
child. Popular, yes—hardly a night passed that
some good-looking boy wasn't ringing the bell
for her.

But Josie wasn't happy. She'd become remote,
distant, and, most alarming of all, she no longer
seemed to care about school.

"Drive carefully, Josie," Rosalie called as she

stood at the door and watched her daughter maneuver the little red Corvette (a sweet-sixteen present from Kermit) down their long, winding driveway.

She watched until the Corvette vanished from sight and then became aware of the mail she was still holding.

Idly, Rosalie shuffled through it. Another invitation from Barbra, this time to raise money to save the cicada. An announcement from Dr. Jared T. Ashkenazy, Plastic Surgeon, heralding the opening of yet *another* office. A letter for Kermit from the Academy.

And something else. A slim, white envelope with a return address that caught her attention immediately: Alumni Affairs, Windsor College, Tinguely, Connecticut.

Her heart began to pound as, with trembling fingers, she tore open the envelope.

CHAPTER TWO

Chrystal

The stupid car door was jammed again. She pushed against it with all her might. When suddenly it opened she half-fell onto the driveway.

The street was pitch dark. The good people of Boonton Harbor were still asleep, dreaming of lottery wins and pots of gold at the end of the rainbow. But people like her, like Chrystal O'Neill Malatesta, couldn't afford the luxury of chasing after rainbows.

Exhausted, she stood on the broken front steps groping for her key. God forbid Vinnie should leave the porch light on. But that would have taken some thought. . . .

From the harbor came the lonely wail of a foghorn. She'd lived here, in this tiny New Jersey waterfront town, all her life, but that sound always filled her with a nameless yearning.

She unlocked the front door and stepped inside. There, on the faded blue couch, in front of the TV, lay Vinnie, her husband of nearly fourteen years. The familiar despair rose within her as she stood there looking down at him. His arrhythmic snoring blended perfectly with the staticky blasts from the TV. In the unreal, flickering glow, Vinnie was a sorry sight, with hair matted, and traces of spittle running down the corners of his open mouth.

She let her eyes travel the length of his body to the empty space where his left foot should have been. She sighed and looked away.

Crushed beer cans littered the floor. Cigarette butts overflowed the pitted ceramic ashtray that Theresa had made in second grade.

A trail of corn curls—extra-crispy barbecue — led from the TV to the couch.

She should leave him. She knew it.

"How can you stand it?" Milt had asked less than an hour ago. "I mean, he hasn't worked in eight years, for crissakes! He gives you nothing but grief!"

"He's given me children," Chrystal said.

Milt grimaced. "It's still no excuse for wasting your life with a lazy bum like him."

Reluctantly, she'd pulled herself from the warmth of Milt's bed. "He wasn't always a bum," she sighed. "It was the accident that changed him."

"How long you gonna blame the accident?"

Milt asked as she edged away. "Hey, Chrystal. Where are you going?" He reached for her again.

"It's almost five-thirty," she reminded him. She stood up and stepped into her uniform. "The kids'll be up soon. Vinnie, too."

Once in the car, she determined again to put an end to this affair with Milton Shrubsole. She hated sneaking around like this. It was wrong.

She'd never meant for things to go this far. She'd never meant to become involved with Milt at all.

It had started innocently enough. One rainy night last April her '72 Chevy had stalled. She'd just come off her shift at the Harbor View All-Night Diner. It was four o'clock in the morning. There she was, standing in the parking lot, getting rained on, and Milt had rescued her. For years he'd been coming into the diner in the middle of the night. He'd suffered from insomnia ever since his wife had died.

"I'll be glad to give you a lift," he offered.

She hesitated. After all, Milt lived on the other side of town. "I don't want you to go out of your way," she protested.

"Don't be silly," he said, holding open the door of his Buick.

To this day she wasn't sure how it had happened. How, instead of driving directly to her little house on Broad Street, they'd somehow ended up at his place overlooking the harbor.

Beethoven was playing on the car radio. That much she remembered. How she loved Beethoven. "I have this album," Milt said. "I'd be glad to lend it to you if you like."

She smiled and nodded. She was ashamed to tell him they didn't own a phonograph. Their old one had given up and there'd been no money for repairs, let alone a new one.

Suddenly just thinking about Beethoven triggered the tears. All the years of hard work at the diner, the worry about the children, the living hand to mouth, and, of course, Vinnie's accident.

Frightened, Milt tried to calm her as best he could. At his place he made her a cup of tea and hovered over her while she drank it.

She was mortified. "This has never happened to me before," she said between sips of the tea.

"Don't worry about it," he said kindly. "Sometimes you just have to let go."

He really was a nice man, she thought, as the tea warmed her. He taught history at the high school. In fact, he was Jace's history teacher. Suddenly she felt uncomfortable.

As if reading her mind, Milt said, "Please don't be embarrassed. If you'd like me to take you home now, I will."

She hesitated. Milt's apartment was small but tastefully furnished. No cigarette butts littered the floor. No crushed beer cans anywhere. She looked at him. And suddenly they were in each other's arms.

That night Chrystal discovered that Milton Shrubsole was not only thoughtful and kind but was also, possibly, the second most wonderful lover in the world.

"You are so-o-o beautiful," he said as he caressed her face, her breasts, her thighs. "If you were my woman, you'd never have reason to cry. . . ."

She found herself responding as much to the words as to anything else. When their lips met—again and again—feelings she thought were dead forever fluttered awake.

Not since Bloom had she known such pleasure.

Who would have thought that shy, unassuming Milton Shrubsole was, as they used to say on the beach at Asbury Park, hung like a Greek god? Adonis would have stepped aside in deference.

Flaccid, Milt's equipment hung halfway to his knee. Erect, he was unbelievably huge. As he entered her endlessly he whispered in her ear, "I want only to please you."

How could he help it? she wondered.

Not since Bloom had she seen a penis of such proportion. Not since Bloom had she had orgasm after orgasm. She and Milt lost themselves

in each other until, at last, she lay spent in his
arms. Then, and only then, when he knew that
she was sated, did Milt at last permit himself to
come.

Afterward, waves of guilt assailed her. Vainly,
she tried to rationalize: She and Vinnie had sex
so infrequently, it hardly counted. And when
they did, the sex was mechanical, perfunctory.
Slam, bam, thank-you-ma'am, and then the
sound of Vinnie's snores.
She was still a young woman. Thirty-four
wasn't exactly geriatric. She had needs. She had
love to give. After the accident she had tried to
give her love to Vinnie, but he had closed himself off, withdrawing within himself so completely . . .

Perhaps it wasn't surprising, then, that she
and Milt should cling to each other. After all,
Milt was lonely. He had loved his wife, Ellie, and
been devastated when he lost her. And so they
fell into a kind of pattern. Three nights a week
he stopped by the diner at the end of her shift
and she followed him in her car, always at a
discreet distance, to his condo by the harbor.
She was always careful to park half a block away.
Milt seemed to treasure the bits of herself she
revealed to him.
One night they had begun by massaging each
other's bodies with oil. Milton had run out of the

expensive mink oil, so they'd had to improvise. They wound up using peanut oil. Carefully, she'd applied it to his testicles.

"Now my nuts smell nutty," Milt chuckled.

"I'm nuts about nuts," she said, beginning to lick the oil from his hot skin. After they'd made especially torrid love, and were lying next to each other comfortably, Chrystal confessed wistfully, "I never intended to become a waitress. I never intended to serve coffee and doughnuts for eight hours every night."

"I figured," Milt replied, his tongue lazily licking the last of the oil from her left nipple.

"I guess I'm the only summa cum laude waitress in Boonton Harbor," she said.

"Summa, huh?" he said as his tongue continued to make lazy circles on her breast.

She nodded, her fingers absently stroking his inner thigh. "Um-hmm," she murmured. "Phi Beta Kappa too. Windsor College. 1974."

She felt his fingers playing peekaboo with her pussy. Even after all that they had done, Chrystal felt herself becoming aroused. Wordlessly, she raised her hips to meet his probing hands.

"Windsor?" he asked, with more than a trace of awe in his voice. The stroking slowed. "My sister tried to get into Windsor and couldn't," he said. "I'm impressed."

In the darkness she sighed. "Don't be. They were the best four years of my life, but they're over now."

Milt sat up. "The best four years, huh? Wanna tell me?"

How could she tell him? She hadn't told anyone about Bloom. How she had loved him. How he had changed her life. But even Bloom had no power over destiny. . . .

She shifted uncomfortably against the pillows. Better not to dwell on what was, she told herself. Especially not while she was in another man's bed, a man who wasn't even her husband.

Now she could see the dawn creeping around the edges of the cheap curtains that covered the bedroom window. She stepped out of her uniform and hung it carefully on a wire hanger. She detested that uniform and all it stood for! But without it, she knew, they would be on food stamps. Or worse. Vinnie's disability payments didn't even begin to cover their expenses.

Her job at the Harbor View All-Night Diner was tedious and backbreaking, but it did have its advantages. On a good night she came home with nearly $100 in tips. Also, by working at night, she had time to be with the kids at breakfast and when they came home from school.

But almost as important, working at night gave her time to write. Without her writing, she didn't think she could survive. The writing was her life, her catharsis. Her salvation.

As soon as she'd finished the last page of *Sweet Awakenings*, she'd begun work on *Making Do*, a sequel, and already her thoughts swirled with plot ideas.

She slipped into her robe and listened. She could hear Vinnie downstairs, hacking and wheezing. The familiar sounds of her husband waking up. Thinking about Vinnie and about what he'd done still made her furious. How could he have been so downright selfish? So stupidly irresponsible? Bad enough he'd taken out a second mortgage without consulting her. But then to gamble away all that money in Atlantic City in a single night! Unthinkable! But then Vinnie always acted before he thought.

"I was hot! I was really hot!" he kept saying over and over again. "I just don't know how it happened, Chrystal. One minute I was on top, and the next, *zip*!" He'd gestured emptily, palms up, looking for all the world like a dazed little boy. And then he'd cried. For days and days he'd sat on the couch and cried.

Chrystal had never known such complete terror. How would they manage? There was no money in the bank. They had bills up to the roof, which Vinnie himself had put on their little house on Broad Street.

The twins were only sixteen months old, Theresa only three. Jace, her Jace, was only five but already in second grade. What could she do? Where could she go? Her mother refused to help.

"You musta done somthin' to make him crazy

like that! I know Vinnie. He's a good boy. Look what he done for you, savin' you from shame like that," her mother had said.

Chrystal was tempted to point out that Vinnie never even knew she was pregnant by somebody else when he married her. But what good would it have done?

Things went from bad to worse to unbearable. Vinnie's depression had deepened until one day he hit bottom. She'd been to the Food Warehouse in Grimsby to stock up on toilet paper and tuna fish. She'd taken the girls with her. When they got home they found the garage door locked. She'd had to go through the house to get in. That's when she found him. Lying on the floor in a pool of blood, his old hunting rifle still in his hand.

Her heart had frozen. "Vinnie!" she screamed.

To her amazement, he opened his eyes.

"Chrystal," he gasped.

She bent over him and cradled his head.

"Chrystal, why is it I can't do nothin' right?"

What he'd tried to do was aim for his brain. What he'd done instead was shoot his left foot to kingdom come. Sheared it clean off at the ankle. How could somebody aim for his brain and shoot off his foot? How like Vinnie!

But his luck hadn't run out completely. At least he was still alive.

That was the good news.

The bad news was, the insurance company refused to pay. "Attempted suicides ain't covered," the stony-faced insurance man told her.

"But it was an accident," she'd lied. "He was cleaning his gun."

"Yeh, and I'm the Queen of Sheba," the man had replied icily.

She looked at her watch. Almost seven. The kids were up now too. She could hear Theresa screaming at Jace to get out of the bathroom so she could get in. Chrystal sighed. If she ever got out of this hole Vinnie had dug for them, the first thing she would do would be to build another bathroom.

Her bones ached. How she longed to soak in a nice warm tub, but that would come later. First came breakfast for the kids. And Vinnie, too, if he was up to it. Then the bath. And then work. Her *real* work.

How long had it been since she'd sent *Sweet Awakenings* to the publisher? Three weeks? No. Three weeks and four days. She knew to the minute when she'd taken it to the post office to mail. Three years of her life had gone into that book. In a way it was like giving birth and sending the baby away.

The kids were halfway through their cereal when Vinnie hopped into the kitchen. He looked like death warmed over. His skin was ashen beneath the night's stubble. His eyes were red-rimmed and filled with defeat.

"I didn't hear you come in this morning," he said, half-accusingly.

"I'm not surprised," she said, not looking at him. "You were out cold."

"Hey," he said, his voice suddenly conciliatory, "I *tried* to wait up. . . ." He hopped over to her and stood too close. His stale breath hit her and she edged away. *"Bella ragazza,"* he murmured groggily, hopping after her as she moved about the kitchen.

Bella ragazza? Beautiful girl? Who was he kidding? Once, maybe, she was beautiful. Once, maybe, her hair had been long and thick and black, her complexion creamy white. What was it Bloom used to say? "A classic beauty . . . a beauty to rival that of the goddess Aphrodite." She shook her head ruefully and elbowed Vinnie away.

"Jesus," he murmured. "What is it with you lately? You act like I got the plague or somethin'."

She sighed. What could she say? That she was at the end of her rope? That if something didn't happen soon, she was going to take the kids and go—where?

If only she could change him! Get him to go out and face the world again! She'd heard about other men who'd lost a hand, a foot, even gone blind, but they still held down jobs, supported their families. Vinnie Malatesta had simply given up.

From the beginning he'd refused to wear the prosthetic. "It looks phony," he'd protested, "and it hurts like hell."

"It takes time to get used to, Vinnie," she'd coaxed to no avail. "Once you get used to it, you can go out and find a job. No one will ever know you're missing a foot. . . ."

But Vinnie was stubborn. Or frightened. Or both. He'd flung the appliance, his shoe still on it, into his closet. "No one would hire me now!" he'd cried. "No one wants a one-footed roofer!"

And so Vinnie just sat. Or he hopped. From the couch to the kitchen from the kitchen to the couch. Back and forth all day long. Eating and watching television and crying into his ever-present beer. Getting fat and fatter until none of his clothes fit him and he took to lolling around all day in his underwear.

"I gotta go, Mom," Jace said, downing the last of his milk.

"What's the hurry?" Vinnie barked. "It ain't even seven-thirty!"

Jace looked at Chrystal through his thick horn-rimmed glasses. "Mom, didn't you tell Daddy?"

"Tell Daddy what?" Vinnie asked, wolfing down the last of the doughnuts she'd brought home from the diner.

"Vinnie, Jace is working on a special science project at school," she said calmly. She paused. She *had* told Vinnie. Three times. But he'd forgotten. Or maybe he hadn't heard her through the beer haze. "His teacher thinks he has a good chance to win the Westinghouse prize. Isn't that wonderful?"

"Westinghouse, huh?" Vinnie said. "The icebox people?"

Jace shook his head. "They make *refrigerators* now, Dad. But appliances are only a fraction of their product output. They're into robotics now. Space technology . . . stuff like that."

Vinnie stared at him. "No shit," he said. "So how 'bout goin' over to Old Man Pollock's after school? I hear he needs kids to help him push those appliances he sells," he said in a slightly mocking tone.

Jace looked hurt. Chrystal threw Vinnie an icy glare. Why couldn't he understand that Jace would never conform to his idea of machismo? Controlling her irritation, she said, "Jace can't do that. After school he has debate team and then there's practice for High School Bowl."

"Gimmie a break!" Vinnie slammed his fist on the table and the dishes rattled. "Why ain't the boy out playin' baseball instead of doin' all that sissie stuff?"

"Because he's got a brain," Chrystal said matter-of-factly. "And because he's going to get into a good college!"

"Oh, sure. A good college like you went to?" Vinnie taunted. "And get his head filled with impossible dreams?"

Eleven-year-old Theresa put her hands to her ears.

Nine-year-old Heather looked up from her bowl of soggy corn flakes. "Do *we* have to go to college, Daddy?" she asked. "Me and Maria?" She pointed to her twin.

Before Vinnie had a chance to answer, Chrystal shouted, "Yes! Everyone in this family is going to go to college!"

Theresa, her eyes filling with tears, begged, "Please don't fight. I hate it when you fight."

Chrystal stood up and began to clear the table. "We're not fighting," she told her daughter. "Now go and practice the piano. You have ten minutes before school."

Without a word, Theresa headed for the piano. Chrystal watched her. She was worried about Theresa. The girl was so ultrasensitive. Shy and introverted. The twins, at least, had each other. Jace had his schoolwork. But Theresa seemed adrift. Chrystal felt a wash of guilt. Life had been hard on Theresa. They'd all been so involved with Vinnie and the problems of survival that Theresa had gotten short shrift. Well, somehow, some way, Chrystal vowed, she'd make it up to her. Last night Chrystal had had a good night at the diner. More than $100 in

tips. Maybe this weekend she and Theresa
would go shopping. K Mart was having a sale.

It was nearly eleven before she sat down at
the typewriter. The same, trusty, secondhand
Underwood that had been a graduation present
from her mother when she'd won the scholarship to Windsor.

From the living room she could hear the
theme song to *Wheel of Fortune*. It was Vinnie's
favorite show, not because he was any good at
word games, but because of Vanna White,
Chrystal suspected. *Vinnie and Vanna*. The perfect couple. Next would come *The Price Is
Right*, and then the soaps. Vinnie wouldn't
bother her for hours.

She inserted a blank piece of paper into the
typewriter and looked around the kitchen for
inspiration. The cheery yellow chrysanthemum
wallpaper lifted her spirits, as usual. It reminded
her of Bloom. Every fall, like clockwork, the
single yellow chrysanthemum would arrive mi-
nus a card. But she knew it was from him.

"My beautiful, my perfect chrysanthemum,"
he'd crooned into her ear as they'd made love
that last time. "So delicate, so incredibly beautiful . . ."

In the cave the moss was soft beneath her.
She'd opened her eyes to see a shaft of golden

sunlight fall onto the cool cave wall, illuminating
the poetry he'd etched there for her:

> The chrysanthemum's amber glow
> Feeds these hungry branches of
> Mine own pure heart . . .

She'd tightened her legs around his undulat-
ing hips and gasped. She could feel him explode
within her, pause, and then, slowly, begin to fill
her again.

"I love you, Bloom," she'd whispered as he
covered her lips with his own. His tongue inside
her mouth was a hot, velvety probe, darting,
licking, sucking her very breath away.

"Don't forget me," she managed to say when,
after making love, they lay side by side on the
moss.

His hand cupped her breast gently. "Forget
you?" he asked. "Does the moon forget to rise in
the heavens? Do the stars forget to twinkle? I
could no more forget you, my sweet chrysanthemum, than forget to breathe."

And he hadn't forgotten her. The birthday
chrysanthemums were proof of that. She had
saved them all, wrapped in tissue and pressed
between the pages of *Lox and Logarithms,* her
favorite book of Bloom's. Fourteen years. Fourteen chrysanthemums.

She shook herself. Sometimes it seemed as
though the past was more real to her than the

present. Better watch it, she told herself. It was
dangerous to get so lost in what can never be
again.

She forced herself to fill the page with words
and was halfway finished when she heard the
wild barking of the neighbor's dog. *The mail-
man!*

She willed herself to remain seated. Don't you
dare move, Chrystal O'Neill Malatesta, she commanded. *A writer is supposed to be immune to
such diversions.*

But the damn dog kept barking. It was impossible to think. Besides, suppose today was the
day she would hear from the publisher? Suppose
today was the day her life would change for the
better? Yielding to temptation, she went to the
front door and opened it.

The mailbox, a miniature replica of their
house made by Vinnie in the early weeks of his
convalescence, was stuffed. The usual junk: a
promo from Magazine Publishers Clearing Barn
promising untold millions if only she would sub-
scribe to their magazines; a flyer from Scrumptious Yogurt with a cents-off coupon and a picture of a beautiful blonde who looked vaguely
familiar; a letter from a collection agency; more
bills. And something else. A slim white envelope
addressed to her: Chrystal O'Neill Malatesta.
The return address: Alumni Affairs, Windsor
College, Tinguely, Connecticut.

Just the words *Windsor College* excited her.

Without hesitating, she ripped open the envelope. An engraved invitation fell into her hand.

You are cordially invited to attend
the retirement banquet honoring
JOSIAH MENDELSOHN BLOOM, Ph.D.

Her knees went weak. The ground tilted. Her dear Bloom retiring?

From inside the house Vinnie called, "Any mail, Chrys?"

"Just the usual," she called back quickly. She slipped the invitation into the back pocket of her jeans and went inside.

On the TV screen Vanna White, clad in a nifty off-the-shoulder jumpsuit, was happily turning letters on the big board. Vinnie couldn't take his eyes off her.

"Hey, get me a beer while you're up, huh?" he asked without turning.

But Chrystal was already back in the kitchen, lost among the chrysanthemums, and she didn't hear him.

CHAPTER THREE

Daphne

The thought of doing it in the office was so deliciously verboten! So undeniably forbidden! Besides, Sid's thick, green carpet reminded her a little of the moss in the cave.

Sidney Funt, M.D., was enjoying himself. His large, capable hands cupped her ass and he groaned appreciatively.

She could tell he was fast approaching the point of no return. They'd been doing it nearly the entire session. As usual, however, she was nowhere near orgasm.

"Squeeze, Daphne, squeeze," Sid panted.

She tightened her vaginal muscles and sighed. What good was all this therapy? she wondered. One hundred twenty an hour twice a week for a whole year, just to learn how to come! Correction. She already knew *how* to come. She'd come lots of times, once. Nine years ago to be exact. But only with one man.

"A classic case of *primary fidelity syndrome*," Sid had diagnosed initially. That was before he, himself, had fallen in love with her. "PFS differs from *nonorgasmic* in a very important way. The body already knows how to respond. It's merely forgotten. . . ."

So he'd attempted to refresh her body's memory—twice a week, on Tuesdays and Thursdays, from 2:00 P.M. to 2:45 P.M. Except, of course, for national holidays or when she was scheduled for a shoot. The holidays she didn't have to pay for; the shoot days, however, came out of her own pocket.

"Daphne, you're learning," Sid groaned as his hips undulated against hers.

"Well, you're a good teacher, Sid," she said, wishing she could be more effusive. What was holding her back? She knew.

Even with Freddie, her late husband, she'd held back, unable to give herself fully. Of course Freddie'd never known that she faked her orgasms with him. But that was history.

That was her trouble. History. Her trouble and her obsession . . .

"My beautiful, my golden daffodil," Bloom had whispered into her ear that last time. "So soft, so delicate, so incredibly wonderful . . ."

Wordlessly, she'd spread her thighs and welcomed him home. "How will I ever live without you?" she wept.

"Oh daffodil," he crooned, "we'll always be a part of each other's memories. . . ."

Sid was panting furiously now. She wondered what time it was, but resisted the impulse to look at her watch. What was it Sid had said? She must clear her mind of all extraneous details.

But it must be close to 2:45. She could tell by the way the sunlight was filtering through the office blinds. She'd been able to know the exact time in the cave, too, just by the way the streams of sunlight had filtered through the opening above them. . . .

"Move faster, Daphne!" Sid ordered breathlessly. "You're losing your concentration!"

What concentration? she wondered. "I'm trying, Sid."

"Try harder!" he gasped, exploding inside of her.

She waited for what she considered a respectable time before sliding out from under him and grabbing for her clothes.

"Daphne, don't rush away," Sid begged. "The session's not over."

"It's getting late, Sid," she said. "Josh will be waiting for me."

"You have time," Sid said.

"He's only a little boy," Daphne called from the bathroom. "It's not fair to make him wait."

She hated Sid's bathroom. Green tile, green towels, even green toilet paper! Sid once explained how the color green was supposed to be psychologically mollifying. Even so, Daphne found it patronizing.

She snapped the crotch of her Donna Karan body suit and stepped into the peach-and-lime Anne Klein skirt. From the outer office she could hear Sid's next patient, the obsessive-compulsive, who always arrived *exactly* five minutes early.

Back in Sid's office, she noticed that he was still only half-dressed and fumbling with the buttons on his shirt.

"Do I look all right?" she asked, smoothing her silky blond hair.

Without looking up, Sid said, "Perfect."

"But you didn't even look!"

He looked. His eyes were brimming with emotion. "Daphne," he explained, "I don't *have* to look at you to see you. I see you every minute of every day. I see you when I'm awake, and I see you in my dreams."

Instinctively, she backed away. Such things frightened her. Men were forever declaring their love for her in one way or another. Not that Sid had actually come out and said the "L" word. But she knew.

"What do you want me to say, Sid? You know how scared I am of commitment. You of all people should know!"

He looked hurt.

"Don't be upset," she pleaded.

"Upset? What makes you think I'm upset?" he said, giving his fly a furious zip. "Daphne, you're never going to get better if you continue to back away from commitment."

She shrugged. "I'm committed. I'm committed to my son. . . ."

The clock on Sid's desk chimed the quarter hour. He was about to say more, but the curtain of professionalism intervened. "We'll talk about this next time, Daphne."

"There may not be a next time," she muttered.

He stared at her, open-mouthed. From the other side of the wall they could hear the obsessive-compulsive scurrying around the waiting room, tidying up the magazines and emptying the ashtrays.

"You don't mean that," Sid said.

She sighed. "I don't know what I mean." It was true. Maybe she should stop seeing Sid. But she needed him. She was so confused. Her life was a mass of tangled threads. The unresolved anger toward her parents, the shock of Freddie's sudden death, the fact that Freddie had died believing that Josh was his. The awesome responsibility of being a single parent. The demands of her career. And, of course, her never-ending love for Bloom. Her secret, solitary, never-ending love for Bloom . . .

"I'll see you Thursday, then?" he asked as she moved toward the door.

"Can't," she said. "We have an all-day shoot at the zoo. Scrumptious is launching a new campaign."

Crestfallen, Sid asked. "Tuesday, then?"

"Maybe," she said noncommittally.

The cab pulled up to the corner of Madison Avenue and Eighty-second Street. She put on her dark glasses and took her place in the crowd of mothers waiting for their children to emerge from the school. She was discovering that being a celebrity had its down side. One of the other mothers was eyeing her right now. "Excuse me," she said. "Don't I know you?"

Daphne shielded her face with her hand. "I guess so. Our kids attend the same school."

But the woman was relentless. "No. From somewhere else. Wait, wait . . . it'll come to me in a minute. . . ."

Fortunately, the bell rang and the kids spilled out. Daphne was dying for a cigarette, but her contract with Scrumptious forbade it. It also forbade grossing out at McDonald's, going into a bar—even a pizza parlor was off-limits. "You're the symbol of health and fitness for an entire generation," warned Elroy Strate, advertising VP for the Scrumptious campaign. "You have a responsibility to the public. That means no junk food, no smoking, no booze."

The *up* side was that Scrumptious was paying her $300,000 a year to eat yogurt on camera and off. *That* she could deal with.

"Hey, Mom!" Josh ran breathlessly up to her.

As always, her heart expanded at the mere sight of him. Would she have told Freddie the truth one day? How could she have? He had loved Josh so. . . .

"Guess what? My class is putting on a play next week and the parents are invited! Thursday afternoon, Mom!"

Daphne's heart plummeted. She hated to disappoint Josh. But what could she do? "Thursday, huh?"

She watched as his expression turned from elation to dejection. "Shit," he muttered softly. "Not another Scrumptious shoot?"

"Afraid so." She nodded.

They started walking slowly eastward. The late afternoon sun burnished Josh's flaming hair to a fiery sheen. Her heart caught. There were moments—and this was one of them—when he reminded her so much of Bloom.

"Why do you have to be the Scrumptious Yogurt Girl anyway, Mom?" Josh asked sullenly.

"You know why. We need the money," she said. But she could understand his disappointment. Poor Josh had a lot of things to be disappointed about. He hadn't wanted to move to the city. He'd made friends in Astoria. Those three cramped rooms above the Laundromat on

Steinway Street were home to him. After all, he'd lived there most of his young life—ever since Freddie's death. It was all she could afford while she looked for work.

Her father, the venerable Austin Windsor Andrews, the "Wizard of Wall Street," had hardheartedly refused to help out. "I warned you not to marry that wastrel in the first place!" he'd raged. "Whose fault is it that the bounder squandered his family's fortune on fast cars and God knows what else? You've made your bed, my girl, and now you have to lie in it!"

Lie in it she did. Seven long years of cheap, garment center showroom modeling, catalog shoots, and even, during a particularly rough dry spell, posing nude at an art school.

And then, like a miracle, "overnight" as they say in the business, she became the Scrumptious Yogurt Girl.

She'd answered a call for a WASPy type for a yogurt commercial. "You got the look, honey," said the casting director. "Straight blond hair, legs up to the *tush,* no tits. *Perfect.* The public will lick it right off their spoons."

That was how she and Josh were able to move back to Manhattan, to the Upper East Side. It wasn't Fifth Avenue, where her parents still lived, but it was close.

"You sure you can't come Thursday, Mom?" Josh persisted as they entered their spacious apartment.

"I can't, baby," she said gently. "Maybe next time. Now go and pour yourself a glass of milk."

She kicked off her shoes and turned on the answering machine. There was the usual call from the agency, confirming the time of Thursday's shoot. Sid, reminding her how important it was to keep her appointments. Her mother, saying she'd gotten tickets for Josh and her to a Little Society concert at Lincoln Center.

Absently, she riffled through the mail. A catalog from I. Magnin. Another bill from Saks. A form letter telling her that her subscription to *Elle* was up for renewal. And a slim white envelope.

She glanced at the return address. What was Alumni Affairs at Windsor College sending her now? Probably another pitch for money. But she'd just sent them a check! She was tempted to toss the envelope, unopened, into the wastebasket. But curiosity got the best of her.

Curiosity and the hope, vague and persistent, that it had something to do with Bloom.

She wasn't disappointed.

CHAPTER FOUR

Bloom

He never meant to fall in love with them. Every year he vowed to render himself impervious to the inevitability of their assaultive charms. But here he was, *again.* In the grasp—literally—of an immovable force.

A delightfully immovable force.

"I don't agree that the nonlover is to be preferred over the lover, Dr. Bloom," Daisy Gabboulian babbled into his ear.

Egad! She was quoting Socrates again! Somewhere along the line, Daisy Gabboulian had gotten the idea that he liked Socrates with his sex.

"Daisy," he said, running his hand over her smooth ass, "let us first of all agree in defining the nature of love."

"Oooh!" she squealed as she guided his fingers between her legs.

"Everyone sees that love is a desire," he recited, reveling in the soft moistness of her pussy.

Momentarily disconcerted, Daisy hesitated. "Oh, Dr. Bloom," she moaned. "I—I—can't seem to concentrate on philosophy and you at the same time."

He diddled with her clit. "Don't worry, my beautiful, my perfect daisy. You are so soft, so delicate, so incredibly wonderful . . ."

"But—but—" she began.

He silenced her with a kiss. Her tongue met his and he moved on top of her. "Don't be upset, my darling Daisy."

With a sigh she said, "Oh, Dr. Bloom. Do we *have* to say good-bye next month when I graduate? How will I ever live without you?"

Where had he heard these words before? He knew. Yet, somehow, his flowers always managed to survive without him. It was never easy for them. Well, come to think of it, it wasn't easy for him, either. In fact, he'd never forgotten any of them. He sent them flowers on their birthdays, didn't he? He kept all their letters, albeit unopened, didn't he?

In spite of himself, his mind wandered. He'd have to pack those letters himself. He musn't forget. In his old age he'd want to read them. . . .

Daisy drew him back to the reality of the moment. Her tongue was drawing lazy circles on his chest and he felt himself respond.

"I love you. You love me. We love each other," she said wistfully.

"Amo, amas, amat," he recited automatically as he entered the sweet depths of Daisy Gabboulian. As he pumped, the familiar roster of Thou-Shalt-Nots poked through the mists of arousal in his brain:

> *Thou shalt not commit adultery.*
> *Thou shalt not hit on thy students.*
> *Thou shalt not put thy reputation*
> *on the line.*

As ever, the devil on his other shoulder paraded the answering excuses:

> *Thy wife is a cold fish.*
> *Thy students beg for it.*
> *Who's to know?*

He shifted uncomfortably above her. He suspected that Douglas Stanley over in Botany knew. He and Doug had been walking across the campus one day last month as Daisy happened by. Old Doug had fondled his pipe lasciviously and leered as Daisy, blond and full-breasted, pretended not to see them. "Isn't she a departure for you, old chap?" Doug had asked.

Bloom decided to play it safe. "She has a fine mind, that girl," he'd said.

Doug had snickered. "Don't give me that fine

mind bullshit, Bloom. You mean fine piece of ass and you know it." Doug had paused and mumbled under his breath, "What they see in you, I don't know. . . ."

Douglas Stanley had headed the Botany Department at Windsor for almost as long as he himself had been head of Philosophy. They had gotten to know each other pretty well over the years, but there was a natural rivalry between them.

But why was he thinking of Douglas Stanley while the glorious Daisy Gabboulian was squeezing his schlong with her pussy?

"Ooooh, Dr. Bloom! Ooooh, it feels so-o-o good! Tell me again how much you want me!"

Tell her how much he wanted her? At this moment he wanted Daisy Gabboulian more than he wanted anything upon this earth. He wanted her more than he'd ever wanted anyone.

Almost.

But this was not the time to think of Estrella DeSouza.

Was there ever a time?

Through the vaulted windows of his Hegel Hall office, the late spring sun shed its warm, muted light upon beautiful Daisy. The door, as usual, was carefully bolted against the chance that one of his students, or even the envious Douglas Stanley, might intrude.

"Josiah, Josiah," Daisy sighed into his ear.

Well, at least she wasn't still calling him Dr. Bloom. It must mean she was nearing climax.

"Take me!" Daisy demanded.

What was she talking about, take her? He was *inside* her! What more did she want?

"Take me to Washington with you!" she screamed for all the world to hear.

Gently, he put his hand over her mouth and tried to calm her. "My darling Daisy, you know how much I love you. But parting is a part of love. Even Juliet knew that, and she was only fifteen."

Daisy nodded.

In truth, he would like nothing better than to have the beauteous Daisy Gabboulian at his side when he was officially proclaimed Philosophical Advisor to the President of the United States of America. But instead of this nubile, sweet-smelling flower of nature, he knew it would be Nora, his barren winter weed of a wife, standing beside him as he accepted the appointment.

He sighed heavily and realized that he had slipped out of Daisy Gabboulian's tight, warm pussy. Not that she noticed. She was beyond noticing. He smiled. He was *that* good. Did they give prizes for fucking? If so, he'd certainly qualify.

He was no stranger to prizes. Twice he had won the Nobel—once in philosophy and once in botany (much to Douglas Stanley's eternal dismay). He'd also won the North American Book

Award three years running for his seventeen
landmark volumes on *The History of American
Thought.* In addition, he'd won the coveted
J.U.L.I.A. for his cookbook, *Lox and Logarithms;* the Coe Award for his definitive treatise
on jogging, *The Endless Lope;* the Rook Trophy
for chess mastery. . . .

So many awards, so many challenges. So much
yet to do. In his middle drawer was the yet-to-
be-completed manuscript of his autobiography,
The Care and Feeding of a Renaissance Man. His
agents were begging him to finish it. He suspected he'd have plenty of time to do just that
once he became Philosophical Advisor to the
President. After all, how much philosophical ad-
vice would a President need? He suspected the
job would require him to be no more and no less
than the twentieth-century equivalent of a
court jester. Of course he would have time to
finish his book.

It would be his most important contribution.
It would also be a catharsis of sorts, because at
last he would tell the world about Estrella.
About his enduring obsession.

Estrella, he thought. *I've come a long way
from the grocery store on Flatbush Avenue, but
I've never forgotten you.* . . .

He wondered what she was doing now, this
very minute. He realized again that he didn't
even know where she lived or whether she was
alive or, God forbid, dead. Never once in all the

years that his name and his picture had appeared in the newspapers and on television had she sent him so much as a postcard. Never once had she called. Never once had she . . .

From a distance he heard Daisy Gabboulian pleading, "Show me! Show me heaven! Show me paradise! Show me . . ."

"You show me yours and I'll show you mine," Estrella said in a singsong voice. Forty years ago, but it seemed like yesterday.

He hadn't even noticed her standing there, in the shadows, behind his father's grocery store on Flatbush Avenue in Brooklyn. He'd gone into the alley for only a moment—just long enough to stack some cases of empties for Papa. He didn't like the alley; it was grimy, fetid, littered with all kinds of garbage too unspeakable to describe. It was no place for a thirteen-year-old Jewish boy bound for Princeton in the fall.

Estrella emerged from the shadows, startling him. He knew who she was, of course. Everybody in the neighborhood knew Estrella DeSouza. "The neighborhood *bummerke*" was how his mother described her. But *bummerke* or not, at sixteen Estrella was the most beautiful girl he'd ever seen.

Not beautiful the way his older sister, Rochelle, was beautiful, with her straight white teeth and her little pointy breasts that wouldn't excite a flea. No. Estrella's teeth were so exqui-

sitely, charmingly crooked, so strangely exciting
in their imperfection. Her mass of unruly black
curls was equally thrilling. More to the point,
Estrella's casaba-like breasts seemed always ripe
for the picking, pulling so provocatively at the
flimsy fabric of the cheap peasant blouses she
wore.

"Hey," she called to him. "You. With the big
nose."

He half-turned. "Who, me?"

"I don' see no one else here wit' a . . ."

"A big nose?"

In spite of the callous words, Estrella's tone
seemed friendly enough.

"Hey," she said again, moving closer. "Is it
true what my brother Ernesto tol' me? Big nose,
big pecker?"

Josiah remained rooted to the spot, too stupe-
fied to speak. "I—I—I don't know what you
mean," he stammered. At Estrella's mention of
the word *pecker,* his own had gone out of control.

Reflexively, he put his hands over his crotch
and tried desperately to think of something that
would make it go down. His mind lit on the
kinetic energy experiment waiting unfinished
in his room upstairs. *No good.* He thought of the
sonata for piano and flügelhorn he'd promised
Herr Pflaumer by Friday. *Still hard as a rock.*
He conjured a vision of his mother and her almost certain heart attack if she could see him

now in the alley with Estrella so close. *Some improvement,* but not much.

Finding his voice at last, he managed, "Wha—what do you want from me? It's getting dark. I have to go . . . I have to get home to work on my experiment." Even to his own ears, it sounded dumb.

" 'Speriment, huh?" she said, cracking her gum. "What are you? Some kinda . . ."

"Scientist?" he finished for her. "You might say that." His pecker was acting up again. He sniffed, taking in Estrella's strange, musky scent. She didn't wear disgusting perfume like his sister Rochelle. He liked Estrella's smell, whatever it was. "I've been accepted into the Institute for Advanced Studies at Princeton." He paused for effect. "I'll be working with Einstein."

She blinked. "No shit," she said. She was close enough to touch now.

"No shit," he echoed, backing up against the brick wall as she slowly, teasingly, lifted her skirt. In the half-darkness her white cotton panties glowed with an otherworldly phosphorescence.

He felt himself getting even bigger. He hadn't known it was possible to get so big. The hundreds of times he'd fiddled with his diddle under the sheet on his hide-a-bed in the dining room, he'd never felt it grow like this.

He looked around frantically. What should he do? Where should he run? And then he realized

that he didn't *want* to run, that he wanted to
stay right here in the alley with the *bummerke.*

"So. Ya gonna show me?" She clicked her
tongue impatiently and unzipped his fly.

"Madre mia!" she exclaimed softly, whistling
through her beautiful crooked teeth.

It was getting hard to breathe. White dots
swam before his eyes. This was all beyond his
wildest dreams. Well, almost. The truth was, in
those secret diddlings of his, Estrella DeSouza
had played a prominent role. All he had to do
was repeat the word *bummerke* a couple of
times and he was done.

"Ernesto was right!" Estrella exclaimed excitedly. "Big nose *does* mean big pecker!" She
licked her lips and smiled at him. In the half-
light the crooked teeth beckoned him. "You
wanna do it?"

He swallowed. "Do it?" He'd better do something. He was supposed to be such a genius, he
couldn't just stand here like a *luksh*, like a wet
noodle.

Almost of their own volition, his fingers slid
inside the white cotton panties. Such incredible
softness! Softer even than Farfel, his sister
Rochelle's white angora cat. A flash of insight
broke through his stupor. *That must be why
they call it pussy!*

Their lips met. A fiery spasm shot through to
the core of Josiah's being as her casabas pressed

against his bony chest. *"Barach atoh, ado . . ."* he intoned.

"Ah do too," Estrella gasped as her hand guided his schlong to that place of Farfel-like softness.

Something had taken possession of him. He was powerless to stop it. Whatever was happening, it was happening faster than the speed of light. His hips were moving against her now like a jackhammer.

By some incredible miracle, he felt himself fusing with this wonderful female. A volcano was building within him. A surging apocalypse. Any minute now it would come.

From afar he heard himself screaming, "It's coming! It's coming!" And then it came.

Was he going to die? Was his heart never going to stop pounding?

Were they both going to die? Estrella was crying as though she'd been wounded.

"Ai dios mio," she wept. "You didn't pull out!"

Trembling, shivering, the sweat beginning to chill his skin, he clung to her like a shipwrecked sailor to a piece of driftwood. What did she mean, pull out?

"You know whatchu done?"

He shook his head wordlessly.

"If you knock me up, they sen' me back to San Juan! They lock me up in de house! Why you do dees to me?"

He was stung. What had he done to make her so miserable? He wished he could comprehend the strange phrases—"pull out," "knock up." Instinctively, he put his arms around her.

"Don't cry, Estrella," he crooned. "I love you, my beautiful, perfect Estrella. . . ."

Amazingly, his words seemed to calm her. He kissed the tears on her smooth, fragrant cheeks.

"If anythin' hoppens, you promise to marry me?" she asked in a small voice.

What could happen? he wondered but didn't ask. He supposed he could marry her. Why not? Someday. But before he could say anything, he heard his father calling from inside the grocery store.

"Josiah, what're you *doing* out there? Digging for gold?"

Panic suddenly overtook him. "I'll be right in, Pa," he called. He glanced at Estrella, who, still in his arms, was looking at him with limpid eyes. "Yes, of course I'll marry you. I love you."

She was *really* staring at him now. "Wait a minute," she said. "How old are you, anyway?"

Should he tell her? People were always thinking he was older than he was, he was so tall. For the past two years he'd had to carry his birth certificate around with him whenever he went to the movies or rode the trolley.

Should he lie and say seventeen? No. "Thirteen," he said.

The gum fell out of her mouth.

Quickly he added, "I'm thirteen, but I'm smart. I can teach you all sorts of things. I'm going to be famous someday. People are going to read about me in the newspaper. I'll give you everything you want. I love you."

Estrella shook her head. "I dunno. I don' rob no cradles. . . ." She paused. "Everything I want?" she asked, chucking him lightly under the chin. "What's your name again?"

He was about to say Josiah, but something, he didn't know what, made him say, "Bloom."

"Bloom." Estrella smiled. "Just like a flower." For a heart-stopping moment, she said nothing more. And then she said, "I love you, Bloom."

"I love you, Dr. Bloom," Daisy Gabboulian crooned into his ear, bringing him back to the ever-present now.

"Josiah, you are *so* wonderful. . . ."

Why did she have to call him Josiah? *Nora* called him Josiah. His cousin Seymour from Pittsburgh called him Josiah. So did his sister Rochelle, for God's sake!

"Bloom," he corrected. "If you love me, call me *Bloom*."

CHAPTER FIVE

The Men

Vinnie wondered what he was going to do without his Chrystal for even a day. *But a whole weekend?*

Damned if he knew. One thing he did know. He was scared shitless that once she stepped onto that precious Windsor campus of hers, she might not ever come home.

Why the hell did she have to go and leave them for three whole days anyway? Why couldn't she have just called Windsor and said she couldn't go—that she had responsibilities at home, that she had four kids and a husband who needed her?

"I think that's everything," Chrystal said, slamming the trunk of her brother Sean's green Dodge.

Vinnie wiped away a speck of soot from the

polished hood of the car. Chrystal's brother spent half his life shining the damn thing. Their own '72 Chevy was again out of commission and sitting on the lawn waiting for him to fix it. Well, this weekend he'd have nothing but time.

Truth was, he had deliberately put off fixing the Chevy in hopes that Chrystal would have no way of getting to Windsor. It was just like Sean, that meddling brother-in-law of his, to throw a monkey wrench into his plans by lending Chrystal the Dodge.

"Remember, Vinnie," Chrystal reminded him, "Jace has debate team after school. He won't be home until five. The girls are at baton practice. They'll be home at five-thirty. So you'll have to start dinner. The water's already on the stove. All you have to do is—"

"I know! I know! Boil the water. Open the box and dump the spaghetti in. I'm not Italian for nothing!"

Absently, he ran his fingers through his hair. Was it his imagination or was he going bald? Jesus H. Christ! That's all he needed! A thirty-five-year-old one-footed ex-roofer with no hair! Not to mention a wife who was preparing to drive off into the sunset, even though it was only eleven in the morning.

"So," he said, trying vainly to think of what else to say. "You think you can manage okay? It's a long drive to Connecticut."

"I can manage," Chrystal reassured him.

He forced a smile. "So you take care, all right? You be sure to call the minute you get there, okay?" Why didn't he just grab her and tell her how much he loved her? How long had it been since he'd told her that? He couldn't remember.

"Uh, Chrystal, honey . . ." he began.

She looked at him, waiting.

He let the moment pass. With one hand on the roof of the Dodge, he hopped over to the door and held it open for her. She seemed surprised.

"Well," she said. "I guess this is it."

He noticed that her eyes were sparkling. She seemed impatient to get started.

Hesitantly, almost as an afterthought, she leaned over and kissed his cheek. "I'll call," she said, patting his hand. Without another word, she slid behind the wheel.

Balancing himself on his one foot, Vinnie watched as Chrystal eased the Dodge smoothly onto the street. He marveled at the way the motor purred. It didn't gasp or cough like the Chevy did—when it was working, that is.

In another minute the Dodge was out of sight. For a second he felt dangerously close to tears. But then, from the house, he could hear the theme of *Wheel of Fortune*. Expertly, he hopped up the front step, with its missing brick, and made it to the couch just in time.

* * *

Milton's mind kept wandering. It had been wandering since that night last month when Chrystal laid it on the line.

"It's no good, Milton. It'll never be any good," she'd told him. "I can't go on like this."

And with that she was out of his life. A whole month. Thirty nights and thirty days. Seven hundred and twenty hours. Forty-three thousand, two hundred minutes. He glanced idly out the classroom window and thought he saw her driving along Claghorn Boulevard.

He was hallucinating, of course, He had been "seeing" her everywhere—in the barber shop, at the supermarket, in the teachers' lounge, even in the men's room. Behind him, Timothy Hanrahan was giving his report on "General Robert E. Lee and ConfedGate." Leave it to Timothy to find smarm and smut in the War Between the States!

He feigned interest, nodding now and then, and smiling. He didn't hear a word. Chrystal filled his brain like high tide in a storm. His gaze returned to the window. He squinted. The woman in the green car looked so much like her! But he knew Chrystal drove a Chevy, a battered old rustbucket if ever he saw one.

But who was he to talk? His own Buick kept stalling every five minutes. In fact, he'd be lucky if he could get himself home when school was out. If three o'clock ever came. Without Chrystal in his life, time was a millstone around his neck, a yoke, a weight.

How was he ever going to manage without her?

Her name was Elizabeth, but everyone called her Biffy. Biffy Barclay. Kermit thought it had a nice shiksa ring to it.

She was something, all right, this Biffele. Straight from the UCLA film school, a real pedigreed thoroughbred with smarts. The kid wanted to be a director.

"Anyone can act," she told him. "Directing. That's where it's at. That's where the power is." Biffy was into power.

In fact, she powered him into taking on *Yesterday's News.* Oy vey! *Yesterday's News* was turning into the biggest mistake of his life. Already they were $14 million in the hole. But was Biffy worried? Of course not.

"So what do you think, Kermit? Antonio goes, right?" She pressed her enormous, perfect tits with their enormous, perfect nipples into him for emphasis.

It was hard to concentrate. The travertine marble desktop was a lot harder than the water bed in her Malibu pad, where he preferred to fuck. But Biffy wanted something new. She was into *new.* In the past six months they'd done it on his office carpet, on the terrace, in the backseat of his car. Today the desk caught her fancy.

"I don't know," he said evasively, thrusting with his hips. He thought he felt something snap in the lower lumbar region but he ignored it. "Antonio's been with me seventeen years. I can't let him go just like that."

"Why not?" She snapped the condom onto him with deliberate intensity. "He's not doing the picture any good. If you took the time to look at the dailies, you'd see that. The light is wrong in almost every frame. . . ."

Kermit winced. He wished she wouldn't talk shop at a time like this. He also wished she wouldn't make him wear a rubber. But his Biffele was into safe sex. She wouldn't even go down on him anymore.

Kermit's gaze fell upon the antique Italian clock Marcello had given him three pictures ago. Eleven o'clock! He gasped.

"Oh, you like that, huh?" Biffy smiled, caressing his balls with her toes.

"No!" he shouted. "I mean, yes! Jesus, how can it be so late? I told Rosalie I'd drive her to the airport!"

Biffy tsked. "Now?" she crooned, her toe lazily noodling his balls. "Right now, this minute, K.O.?"

He loved it when she called him "K.O." It made him feel like Jake LaMotta. "I'm sorry, babe. I don't want to make her suspicious." But he knew that Rosalie was already suspicious. He'd almost *plotzed* that morning when she'd

asked who Elizabeth Barclay was. He'd
phumfeted something. "A shiksa with big
boobs," he'd almost said. "A shiksa with big
bucks," he *did* say. But he knew she knew, even
if she didn't know what she knew.

He told Biffy, "She'll be gone all weekend.
We'll check into the Shangri-La in Santa Monica
and fuck for forty-eight straight hours."

The thought should have thrilled him. So why
did he feel so lousy? Because Rosalie was going
away, that's why. They'd been married seventeen years and he didn't even know if he loved
her anymore. So why did he get depressed every time she went away for even a day?

Reluctantly, Biffy slid off him. She was pissed,
and he couldn't blame her. He sat up. A sharp
pain shot through his back.

Alarmed, Biffy asked, "What is it?"

"Nothing," he gasped.

It took him twenty minutes just to schlep himself from the studio to the car. By the time he
drove up the winding driveway of their home
on Butterjay Lane in Beverly Hills, he was in
true agony.

Rosalie was waiting outside for him.

"Kermit? You're late! What took you . . . ?"

"Nothing," he lied. "Get in."

She tossed her suitcase in the back and slid in
beside him. In spite of himself, he had to give
her credit. For an old broad of thirty-eight she

didn't look half bad. In fact, she looked damn good.

"It's your back, isn't it?"

How did she know? Because she knows me, Kermit told himself. She knows me and she loves me. "Don't worry about it," he said.

"Are you sure you're okay?"

He wasn't sure. Suddenly he wasn't sure of anything. He felt tempted to tell her everything. But how could he? He was her whole life, her knight in shining armor. It would break her heart if she knew he hurt his back *shtupping* Biffy Barclay.

They drove for a while in silence. And then she said, "Kermit, we have to talk."

He groaned inwardly. *Again* talk? The last thing he wanted to do was talk.

"About Josie," Rosalie said.

He felt a surge of relief. Josie, he could talk about.

"Something's bothering her," Rosalie said. "Last night I heard her crying herself to sleep. Promise me you'll have a talk with her while I'm gone. God knows, she won't talk to me."

He nodded. "Sure, sure," he said. The spider-like structure of LAX loomed in the distance. He'd be only too happy to talk with Josie. He loved her like his own. But then again, what did he know from teenagers? But then again— wasn't Biffy Barclay practically a teenager?

The idea caught him short. And then they were there.

"I'll call when I can," Rosalie said, leaning over to peck his cheek.

He strained forward and grimaced in pain.

"It's really bad, huh?" Rosalie said, watching him.

He waited for her to say she would cancel her trip, that she was going to stay home and tend to him, her husband, the light of her life, and forget this Windsor College nonsense.

Instead, she said, "You take it easy, Kermit," and bent to fetch her bag from the back of the Ferrari.

Why did Daphne have to be so happy? Sid wondered.

Not once this year had he seen such elation on her beautiful face. Most of the time she was either preoccupied, or worried, or both. He supposed he should be happy that she was happy. And he would be, if only her happiness had to do with him—Sidney Funt, M.D. But he suspected that glow on her face had nothing to do with him and everything to do with this trip to Windsor.

"You sure you can handle a shift?" he asked for the umpteenth time. He put his hand over hers on the stick and went through the motions again.

She clicked her tongue. "Sid, how many times

do I have to tell you? I was married to a race-car driver! Freddie taught me all there is to know about gearshifts!"

He made a face. *Freddie again.* "Those were racing cars," he sneered. *"This* is a Land-Rover! The Queen of England drives one!" he said with pride.

Daphne rolled her eyes. "Look, Sid," she said. "If you're so uptight about lending me the car, I'll take the train. . . ."

He shook his head. Uptight? How dare she call him uptight? "Daphne, you're missing the point," he said. "I *want* to lend you my car. It means a lot to me. *You* mean a lot to me. *I want to.*" The truth was, he'd never lent his car to anyone before. That he was willing to lend it to Daphne must mean something. Perhaps he really *was* in love with her. Perhaps it was more than just doctor-patient relations.

The thought frightened him. He'd have to go into this in depth with Reinisch next session.

"Promise me you'll call when you get to Tinguely," he said, unfolding the list of automotive do's and don'ts he'd prepared.

"Sid, I'll try, but I'm not promising," she said stubbornly.

Why couldn't she promise? he wanted to know. Because she had as much trouble making commitments as he did, that's why.

They sat in silence for long moments. He couldn't think of anything else to say. Why did he find it so hard to say good-bye? It was that old separation bugaboo again. It was his mother's fault. It had to be. She had toilet trained him too early. That was it.

In desperation he said, "Daphne, it would be no big deal for me to come with you."

She looked surprised. "What about your patients, Sid?"

He shrugged. "The compulsive overeater would be only too happy for an excuse to binge. The manic-depressive is on a high, he wouldn't even notice I'm gone. . . ."

She put her hands to her ears. "Sid! I won't hear of it!"

Grasping at straws, he said, "What about little Joshie? Don't you think three whole days is a long time to leave him with those neurotic parents of yours?" It was a low blow, he knew, but it was his only resort.

She looked stricken. "Dr. Sidney Funt! Aren't you always telling me to stop being such an overprotective mother? Besides, Josh *loves* my parents. . . ." But she sounded uncertain.

He was ashamed of himself for being desperate enough to try and lay a guilt trip on her. *What was the matter with him?*

Suddenly that old Beatles tune popped into his head, something about letting your girl drive your car if you loved her. "Baby, you can drive my car," or something.

Of course! It was as clear as the nose on his

face! He *did* love Daphne! He loved her more than he'd loved anyone, ever.

So why couldn't he tell her? Just come right out and say it? Those three little words?

He handed her the keys. "Please drive carefully," he said.

Damn. The *wrong* three little words!

His next session with Reinisch was going to be a doozy!

PART TWO
Coming Together

CHAPTER SIX

Bluma

She couldn't stop crying. Everything had gone wrong from the minute she'd left San Juan. First, the plane was two hours late taking off. Next, the weather forced them to set down in Houston instead of New York.

Maybe that was where they'd lost her luggage. She'd been standing at the carousel here at Kennedy Airport for almost an hour and her suitcase still hadn't appeared. The thought of losing that beautiful burnished-leather suitcase was unbearable. Her papa had given it to her as a high school graduation present.

Well, at least she still had her carryon, a gift from her darling *abuelita,* her grandmother, who'd practically raised her.

Bluma fished in the carryon for a tissue. The tears just wouldn't stop. All around her people were meeting and kissing and leaving with their luggage. She wished her Aunt Lina and Uncle Ernesto had been able to meet her here and drive her up to Tinguely, Connecticut. But they both worked hard all day, and besides, their car was too old to make the trip.

She tried to pull herself together by telling herself how lucky she was to have won the scholarship to Windsor College. Lucky, too, to have gotten an on-campus summer job in the Elias Windsor Hall and Dining Facility. She was to start tomorrow morning.

Would she get there in time? She looked at her watch. It was already 11 P.M. No wonder she was starving. There'd been a meal on the plane, but she'd been too excited to eat.

She saw a burly guard in a blue uniform watching her. Meekly, she approached him. "Excuse me, sir . . ."

The man raised an eyebrow. "Can I help you, miss?"

"My suitcase," she began. "I think it's lost." She hated the childish whine in her voice, but she couldn't help it. She was hungry and tired and felt so all alone.

The guard was about her father's age—fortysomething. He was staring down her blouse. She looked away.

"Yeah, well, that kinda thing happens all the time," he said. His voice was oily and creepy. "Don't you worry, honey." Without another word, he slipped his hand around her tiny waist and led her across the terminal to a small, glass-walled office. He rapped on the glass. "Hey, Charlie, we got us a lady in distress."

Charlie yawned and pushed some papers toward Bluma. "Describe the lost article, give your flight number and point of departure and destination . . ." he said mechanically.

Bluma wished the guard would take his hand off her waist. She could feel his fingers beginning to inch their way down to her behind. She wished Papa was here. He'd take care of this jerko.

With more confidence than she felt, she moved away from the guard and said, "Thank you. I think I can manage from here."

"You shouldn't be alone in an airport like this," he said. "I'll stick around and take care of you."

Quickly she improvised. "My whole family is meeting me," she lied. "My uncle and aunt and four big cousins. They're probably waiting for me right outside."

He smirked as if he didn't believe her.

"Beat it, willya, Winston!" Charlie yelled from inside the glass enclosure. "Leave the poor kid alone!"

Winston threw up his hands as if to say, "Who, me?" But he walked away.

Bluma gave Charlie a smile of gratitude.

* * *

Once outside, she shivered in the chill night air. Although it was the end of May, the weather up here was colder than she ever would have believed. The thin peasant blouse her *abuelita* had made her especially for the trip was no protection at all, and all her sweaters were in her lost suitcase.

She read again the printed directions the school had sent to her. She was to take the airport bus to Grand Central Station in Manhattan, New York City. From there she was to take the Amtrak train to Hartford, Connecticut.

In Hartford her Uncle Ernesto would meet her and take her to his house, which was in Tinguely, Connecticut, where Windsor College was.

All those strange-sounding places! It was all so confusing! How would she know which bus to take? Which train? She looked around. So many cars and buses and taxis too. Even long, shiny limousines, like the one that was pulling up right in front of her. She watched, shivering, as the driver got out and held up a sign: "Mrs. Kermit O. Fineberg." How fortunate Mrs. Kermit O. Fineberg was, whoever she was, to have a beautiful, shiny limousine waiting for her.

She tried to convince herself that she, Bluma DeSouza, was lucky too. She was the first college girl in her entire family. Not even her wonderful papa had been to college, even though he was the smartest man she'd ever known. There were people who said that José DeSouza was a genius, that he could fix any television set in any hotel in San Juan—in any hotel in the whole world, for that matter. She was going to miss him very much, her papa with the flashing dark eyes and crooked teeth and wonderful red hair.

She felt close to tears, but she promised herself she would not cry.

She watched as an attractive, beautifully dressed woman came out of the terminal and approached the limousine. Immediately the driver snapped to attention and rushed to take her suitcase.

"Good to see you again, Mrs. Fineberg," the driver said, holding the door open.

"How are you, Henry?" the woman asked. "I hope you haven't been waiting too long."

"No, ma'am. Just got here. The traffic on the Long Island Expressway is not to be believed."

"Some things never change," the woman said as she slid gracefully into the limousine. "Are we going to take the Whitestone or the Throgs Neck Bridge to Tinguely?"

Bluma gasped. "Tinguely, Connecticut?" Bluma blurted before she could stop herself.

The woman and the driver both stared at her.

Quickly, Bluma explained, "I'm going to Tinguely, Connecticut, too. I'm going to be a student at Windsor College. I have a job waiting for me in the Elias Windsor Hall and Dining Facility."

Mrs. Fineberg smiled. "Now that's a happy coincidence," she said. She looked around. "Are you waiting to be picked up?"

Bluma once again felt the sting of tears. "I'm supposed to call my uncle when I get to Hartford, Connecticut, and he's going to pick me up there," she said very softly. Her *abuelita* had warned her against talking to strangers. But she was tired and cold, and she wanted a ride very much.

"I'd be very happy if you joined me," Mrs. Fineberg said graciously. "I'm a Windsor girl too."

The driver asked, "Where's your luggage?"

"They lost it," Bluma murmured. "All I've got is my carryon."

"Poor lamb," Mrs. Fineberg said, patting the seat beside her. "Don't worry. We'll get you to Windsor and I'm sure they'll find your luggage tomorrow."

For the first time since she'd left home, Bluma felt safe. Someone else besides her *abuelita* and Papa seemed to care what happened to her.

CHAPTER SEVEN

Chrystal

Sean's precious old green Dodge had brought her across two hundred miles of bridges and highways without a glitch. And now, just as she was approaching the Tinguely exit—she could actually make out the outline of Andrews Chapel against the hazy twilit sky—she heard the loud blam that signaled a flat!

Damn!

Resignedly, she pulled to the side of the road and got out to investigate. Cars whizzed by her with alarming speed.

"Hey, lady! You tryin' ta cause a major accident?" some nut screamed as he caroomed within inches of the Dodge.

Trembling, she inched her way around the car. It was the left front tire. Flat as a flapjack! She had no idea in the world how to fix a flat. She didn't even know if Sean had a spare. She unlocked the trunk and saw to her dismay that, indeed, he didn't. Her heart sank. What to do?

Then she remembered what Jace had said that very morning before he'd gone off to school. "Be careful driving, Mom. And if anything happens, don't panic. Just sit tight, lock all the doors, and wait for the state troopers. They'll come along sooner or later."

God bless Jace! So wise and so knowing. So like his father . . .

She got back into the car and leaned against the seat. The doors were locked. All she had to do was wait.

She was so near, she could almost feel his presence. Would he have changed in the fourteen years they'd been apart? Would he recognize her? She remembered his voice—so deep, so resonant, so soft and caressing. . . .

She closed her eyes. What a brilliant man. What a brilliant teacher. . . .

"Professor Bloom, what would Plato have said about Watergate?"

There was a ripple of amusement in the lecture hall. Shirley Peppermill—Peppi to her friends—the senator's daughter, remained standing until Bloom motioned her back into her seat.

The lecture hall was jammed, as usual—at least four hundred girls. But not a sound was heard as they all waited for Professor Bloom to speak.

He paced back and forth in thoughtful consideration. To look at him, no one would guess at his brilliance. He was tall, but not *very* tall. Not very handsome, either. A cloud of unruly red hair framed a thin big-nosed face. But his piercing blue eyes seemed to see—and know—everything.

It was his very lack of "pretty boy" looks that made Professor Bloom so appealing, so "ordinary," and yet so extraordinary.

"In the quest for Truth," he began, "there are numerous detours."

A palpable silence settled in the room. Four hundred pairs of eyes followed him as he paced back and forth, lost in thought.

"It is my belief that Plato might have considered Watergate just such a detour. . . ."

A sea of hands shot up, waving wildly for attention. Chrystal sat quietly while all around her girls were murmuring among themselves about the latest twist in the Watergate scandal.

"Miss O'Neill, any thoughts?"

A hush fell once more over the crowded hall. Chrystal felt the blood rush to her head. How could he know her name? The semester had only just begun. Why had he singled her out?

Shakily, she stood. "Well," she began, clearing her throat. "I—I—I'm sorry, Professor Bloom, but, uh . . ." Should she say what she really thought? She glanced at Peppi Peppermill.

"Yes, you . . ." he prodded.

She swallowed. "Professor Bloom, I think you're evading the issue."

A chorus of gasps echoed throughout the room. Chrystal's heart pounded wildly. Although she was a senior, this was the first opportunity she'd had to take a course with the fabled Professor Josiah Mendelsohn Bloom. By answering him as she had, had she committed an unpardonable faux pas?

"Professor Bloom," she continued with more confidence than she felt, "you seem to assume that Nixon *was* seeking Truth. I happen to believe that Nixon was seeking deception."

More gasps. When would she learn to keep her political views to herself? She should know better. Shirley Peppermill's father was practically one of Nixon's accomplices. The senator's daughter was glaring at her now with open hatred.

Professor Bloom was smiling at her! It was a dazzling smile. He was better-looking than she'd thought.

Now his index finger was wagging playfully at her. "Ah," he said. "But, Miss O'Neill, *that* is *your* opinion. The original question was, 'What would *Plato* have said?'"

The other girls giggled gleefully.

"He's got you now, O'Neill."

"Sit down, Chrystal," urged Feather Goodey, the tin-mine heiress who was Shirley Peppermill's best friend. "Go back to the boonies!"

Gales of laughter this time.

The rest of the lecture was a blur. Maybe it was a mistake for her to have come to Windsor after all. She didn't really belong here with all these rich men's daughters. Her own father had died of a heart attack on his fishing boat when she was only three. Her mother had supported them by giving permanents and manicures in their kitchen. Maybe she should have gone to Boonton Harbor Community College and learned data processing.

She was halfway across the campus when she felt a hand on her arm. She looked up in surprise. Professor Bloom!

"Miss O'Neill, may I have a moment?"

She hugged her books to her chest. Why did he want to talk to her? Would he have her suspended because she implied that Richard Nixon was a crook? Or was he merely offended that she had implied he was being evasive?

"I'm sorry if I offended you, Professor Bloom," she said, "but I still—"

"Please," he begged. "Won't you call me Bloom?" He slipped his hand under her elbow. "Let's go to the Tinguely Inn for a cup of coffee."

It wasn't a request. To her own surprise, she found herself eager to follow him.

When they were seated across from each other in a booth, he smiled. "You've no idea how refreshing it is to hear someone speak her mind. I've been 'yessed' to death by young women who say only what they think I want to hear. How foolish of them." He sighed.

She nodded. Then she caught herself. She didn't want to "yes" him. But she didn't want to "no" him, either. She didn't know what she wanted.

It wasn't too long before she found out.

She was trembling. She was burning. She'd never felt this way before. How could she help but fall in love with this marvelous man?

For the first time she truly understood what Truth and Beauty were all about. They were not just words, not mere concepts. They were life itself, and they flourished here, in this cave that he had led her to only moments before.

The morning had begun routinely enough. At nine o'clock sharp she was already in his Hegel Hall office, typing his lectures as she had every Saturday morning for the last month. Today she intended to proofread a paper he was to read before the Hartford Philosophical Society.

But he was already in the office, pacing back and forth in front of the high, vaulted windows. He seemed preoccupied, frowning, definitely troubled.

"Oh," she'd said, seeing him. "I hope I'm not

disturbing you, Professor. But I thought I'd get a head start on that paper for the Society. . . ."

Bloom looked at her as if seeing her for the first time. "You know, you're really quite beautiful," he said.

Her heart flipped inside her chest. Before she could say anything, he held up a hand and apologized. "I know I have no right to speak to you like this. Go ahead. I'll leave you to get on with your work."

"I can do it some other time," she said, letting her voice trail. Her mind was filled with questions. What had brought him here so early? Was it a personal problem? She had heard the rumors that Professor Bloom and his wife weren't getting along. Was that it? She pictured his wife —a thin, sour-looking woman. Nora, that was her name. Perhaps they'd had an argument. Perhaps that was why he looked so miserable.

Bloom sighed. At the door he seemed to hesitate. "Listen," he said. "I know this sounds crazy, but would you care to run with me today?"

"Run?" she asked. Then she remembered that Professor Bloom was a marathon runner and author of *The Endless Lope,* the quintessential handbook on jogging.

"Maybe it's not a good idea, after all," he said. "If you'd rather not, I'll understand."

"No, no . . ." she began. "I'd love to run with you. I can't think of anything I'd rather do."

The leaves were turning. Crimson and gold waves lit up the Tinguely countryside like a fiery sea. She jogged behind him up the sloping foot-hills surrounding the campus. He was more than twice her age, but she had trouble keeping up with him.

"You all right?" he called over his shoulder from time to time.

She nodded, lacking the breath to answer. It was all she could do to keep him in sight. She suspected he was pacing himself to accommodate her.

When they finally stopped she was grateful.

He turned to her. "Exhilarating, isn't it?" he asked. He was definitely looking happier. The sadness had left him and a boyish exuberance had taken its place.

If only she could catch her breath!

He was watching her closely. "Running takes a little getting used to," he admitted. "I think this is enough uphill for today."

Wordlessly, he took her hand. "Chrystal," he said. "Lovely name. *Chrystal.* Chrysanthemum. Sweet and honest." He looked at her. "Refreshingly bright."

Her breath was coming back now. But she was still unable to speak. What could she say to him that wouldn't sound foolish or, worse, dumb?

He gestured widely. "Have you ever seen such beauty?" The Windsor College campus was spread out in concentric circles below them.

The buildings looked like toy houses on a majestic game board of golds and reds.

She looked around.

"We're on Bush Hill," he told her shyly. "Don't tell me you've never come up here before with a young man?"

She hadn't. There were many things she hadn't explored in her four years on campus. She was always too busy—studying, working, trying to get as much out of college as she could because who knew if she'd ever be able to go on to graduate school.

"This is a beautiful spot," she acknowledged.

He fixed his piercing blue eyes on her. She felt herself blush. . . .

One minute they were standing together on the bluff. The next, they were naked in the cave.

"Welcome to my sanctuary," Bloom had whispered as he led her through an almost unnoticeable crevice between two enormous boulders.

It was an entrance to another world.

Chrystal was amazed to find herself in a cathedral of stone. The walls rose in an almost perfect arch. A brilliant swath of sunlight fell from above where the rocks did not quite come together. It was as though God's hand had formed this ethereal haven just for them.

The ground was covered with a soft, pale moss. The walls were smooth and cool to the touch. From somewhere far above Chrystal heard the sweet, pure sound of a bird. She felt an incredible sense of serenity in this secret chamber of Professor Bloom's.

"How did you ever find . . ." she began.

"This wonderful place?" he finished. "I happened on it quite by accident," he said wistfully. "When I was very young. A lifetime ago."

Standing so close to him in the cave, she began to feel light-headed. She felt the ground begin to move beneath her feet. She felt herself swoon. And then his strong arms took hold of her and drew her closer to him.

She lifted her face to his. She closed her eyes. She felt his lips upon hers. Fire built within her as their tongues met. . . .

It was wrong and she knew it. He was a married man. He was her *professor*. Still, how could something that felt so incredibly right be wrong?

Her flesh burned beneath his searching fingers. When he guided her hand to his zipper she froze.

"Please," he begged. "My beautiful, bright chrysanthemum—I need you so much!"

She felt herself melt all over again. This man had orchestrated summit meetings, had twice won the Nobel Prize. The very thought that he needed *her*—Chrystal O'Neill, a scholarship student from a New Jersey shore town—was almost inconceivable. Nevertheless, for some unknown

reason he had chosen her out of all the women
on earth. Who was she to question?

"My wife doesn't understand me," he said,
reaching under her sweater and deftly un-
hooking her bra.

She responded to the misery in his voice.
What irony. Such a great man, yet all his accomplishments had failed to bring him happiness.

He sank to his knees and pulled her down
onto the moss with him. They kissed again. And
then, slowly, he lifted her sweater over her head
and gasped.

> "Thy white milky orbs
> Blind me with their luminescence
> Casting shadows upon all else . . ."

And then his mouth closed on her nipple.

She sucked in her breath. And then she
moaned. "Ohhh—ohhh—Professor Bloom—"

In another moment her jeans lay crumpled in
a corner of the cave. "Sweet, sweet chrysanthemum," he panted as he fumbled with his own
zipper. "Call me Bloom."

"Bloom, oh, Bloom," she moaned as his
tongue slid along her inner thigh and came to
rest on her secret parts. "Ohhh, Bloom, Bloom
. . . BLOOM . . ."

Hurriedly he mounted her. Beneath him, she
felt herself thrashing wildly, opening herself to
him totally.

"My sweet chrysanthemum, my perfect flower . . ."

"I love you, Bloom," she murmured. "Love you, love you, love you . . ."

From far off she heard the rhythmic tap-tapping of a branch against the outer wall of the cave.

"Ma'am? Ma'am! You okay in there?"

She awoke with a start, her body stiff and aching in the cramped front seat of the Dodge. A young trooper was staring at her through the windshield. Quickly she rolled down the window. "I have a flat," she explained. "There's no spare."

"I'll call road service," he said. "You wait here. Where're you heading?"

She pointed into the darkened distance. "Windsor," she said. "I'm going back home to Windsor."

CHAPTER EIGHT

Rosalie

It had been so long since she'd seen the campus. The last time was in 1971, when she'd graduated. Three weeks pregnant with Josie, though she didn't know it then.

Seventeen years ago.

The limousine pulled up in front of Elias Windsor Hall and Dining Facility. "This is fine," she told Henry. Bluma DeSouza was still asleep on the seat beside her. Rosalie hadn't the heart to wake her. Such a pretty young girl. So sweet-natured. Bright, too. Such beautiful thick dark hair. Wild, untamed hair. She'd worn her hair like that once. . . .

"Get with it, Samotsky," urged Cathy Smythe, Rosalie's freshman roommate. "Brillo hair is out. Smooth is in. Why don't you let me iron that orange mess for you?"

Rosalie looked up from her book. Cathy was a ringer for Nancy Sinatra in her white Courrèges boots, her white suede miniskirt, and her matching fringed vest. Her smooth black hair was long and parted in the middle, just like Nancy's. Right for Cathy, maybe. Not so right for Rosalie.

"Please, Cathy," Rosalie pleaded. "Can't you find someone else's hair to iron?" She'd gone back to rereading Bloom's new book on the metaphysical connection between the ingestion of smoked salmon and mathematics *(Lox and Logarithms)*.

"Suit yourself," Cathy said, slamming the door.

And she did.

The next year—and for the rest of her tenure at Windsor College—Rosalie opted for a single room. A cell-like room in Egmont Hall, commonly known as "Egghead Acres" because of the grinds and other misfits who chose to live there.

Even though the room was small, she cherished it because it was hers. Hers alone. At home in Bakersfield she'd had to share a room with Tante Rifka, her grandmother's unmarried sister. She and Tante Rifka were roommates until Tante Rifka died at the age of ninety-seven the year before Rosalie graduated from high school.

It was no wonder, then, that she reveled in her privacy.

Even privacy had its limits, however. From

time to time she'd attended a mixer or two. There was just one problem: The boys who came to Windsor College mixers were just that —boys. Out to have a good time. Which meant just one thing—*scoring. Making it. Nooky.*

Call it what you will, Rosalie wasn't interested.

Not that she was a virgin. Thanks to Melvin Findlestein, son of Herman Findlestein, her parents' insurance man. She and Melvin had one important thing in common: Their parents didn't understand them. Melvin wanted to be an astronomer and his father was *nudging* him to be a doctor. "Pop can't understand that there are other kinds of scientists," he complained. "Doesn't he know that any schmuck who can memorize can become an M.D.?"

Melvin looked up at the stars in Rosalie's backyard. "That's where it's at, Rosalie," he said dreamily. "That's where all the answers are. Up there."

Rosalie sighed. "Not all the answers, Mel," she'd said. "We can still learn a lot from Socrates and Aristotle . . . and Bloom."

Melvin, sitting close to her on the back steps, looked puzzled. "Bloom?"

"Josiah Mendelsohn Bloom," she said. "The philosopher. I've read everything he's written. I want to be a philosopher. My father wants me to learn typing and shorthand."

Melvin nodded. "Maybe that's not such a bad

idea," he began. Then, seeing the stricken look
on her face, he amended hastily, "I mean, I
mean . . . shorthand will come in handy in college. . . . You can take notes. . . ."

It was May. High school graduation was still a
month away. They were both on the precipice
of life—she bound for Windsor, he for Harvard.
Suddenly, Melvin inched closer. "You want to do
it, Rosalie?"

The question took her by surprise. She
couldn't think of any reason to say no, which was
why she nodded yes.

So they did it. Right there. In the backyard.
Under the stars. From the house they could hear
the theme music to *The Jackie Gleason Show*
and knew that her parents wouldn't bother
them for at least an hour. . . .

The boys here, the ones who came to the mixers, were nothing like Melvin, who still wrote
her letters from Harvard, where, after all, he
was a premed student. Melvin was sensitive and
intelligent and kind. These boys, who came
from nearby schools like Lodge College and
Hartpence University, were callous, calculating,
and shallow. Worse, they were snobs. That's why
Sheldon Grasch was such a surprise.

She met Sheldon through Mindy Epstein,
who had the room next to hers in Egmont Hall.
One Friday night Mindy, frantic, red-faced, at
her wit's end, practically broke down Rosalie's
door. "Rosalie, please, *please!* Arnie's best friend

Sheldon's date has mono and we have tickets to hear Timothy Leary. You've got to come with us. *Please.* Sheldon will be perfect for you. I know it!"

Rosalie was in the middle of Volume XII of Bloom's *History of American Thought.* It was fascinating. "I don't know, Mindy," she said uncertainly.

Mindy rolled her eyes. "It's Friday night, for God's sake! Even *you* deserve a break! Rosalie— I'll do your laundry for a month if you say okay!"

Rosalie considered. She hated doing laundry. It was only for an evening, after all. How bad could this Sheldon be?

To her utter astonishment, he wasn't bad at all. He was, in fact, perfect. A grad student at Hartpence, Sheldon was tall, bearded, and gorgeous. Not to mention brilliant. He'd already published two slim volumes of poetry. His specialty was Rimbaud. She fell in love with him immediately.

For three weeks she was totally ecstatic.

But then came the fourth week. They'd been to the Tinguely Arts Cine and were walking back to campus. It was early November, and the night air was cold. She shivered. She glanced at Sheldon. Something was bothering him, she knew. He'd hardly said three words all night.

The clock on the spire of Andrews Chapel bonged eleven times. Sheldon seemed relieved. "Gee, it's getting late," he said.

"I don't have any early classes tomorrow," she said.

"Well, I do," he said, reluctantly letting her draw him to a bench.

They sat down together.

In the three weeks they'd been dating, Sheldon had yet to kiss her. This evening she had carefully brushed her teeth and eaten half a roll of breath mints. She appreciated the fact that Sheldon wasn't after her body, but enough was enough. She took his fingers and pressed them to her lips.

He squirmed uncomfortably.

"What's wrong?" she asked.

"Rosalie," he said. "I have something to tell you."

Her heart plummeted. Whatever he was about to tell her, it wasn't going to be good.

"It's another girl, isn't it?" she said, her voice cracking.

"No! No!" Sheldon said hurriedly. "It's not a girl."

She almost fainted from relief. But if it wasn't another girl, what was it? She looked up at him with questions in her eyes.

He shook his head. "God, Rosalie, this is so hard for me. . . ."

Hard for him? What did he think she was going through? She tried to smile. "Whatever it is, Sheldon, I'll understand."

But she didn't understand. She would never understand.

"Do you remember my date who had mono?" he asked her.

She nodded.

"Well, he's better now. His name is George. I saw him today and we're getting an apartment together."

It was as though someone had knocked the wind out of her. She had trouble breathing. She got up and her feet buckled under her.

"God, Rosalie," Sheldon whispered as he helped her up, "I never meant to hurt you. I like you. You have a really fine mind. You—"

But she didn't stay to hear the rest. She ran as fast as she could into Egmont. But Sheldon didn't follow.

The next day, and the day after that—and for still another day—she refused to leave her room. Rosalie Samotsky, the girl who'd never missed a day of school in her life, didn't think she would ever leave her room again. She had loved Sheldon with all her heart. Why hadn't he been able to love her?

Perhaps nobody would ever love her. Perhaps she was unlovable. . . .

On the fourth morning Mindy Epstein rapped at Rosalie's door.

"There's someone downstairs to see you," she said. Mindy sounded as though she'd been crying too. Yesterday afternoon she'd brought Rosa-

lie tea and toast. "I had no idea he was a fag,
Rosalie," Mindy had said, looking miserable and
guilty. "Arnie swears he didn't know, either. You
have to eat something, Rosalie. You can't make
yourself sick over something like this."

So Rosalie had taken a sip of the tea. Her
hands had trembled so badly that she spilled
more tea on her robe than she drank. She
couldn't help feeling that if she were more
womanly, more beautiful, less of what her father
called a *meeskite,* Sheldon wouldn't have gone
back to George.

Mindy had taken a bite of Rosalie's untouched
toast. How was it that Mindy, barely five feet tall
and nearly as wide, could find someone to love?
She and Arnie had been together for months.

"Honest, Rosalie," Mindy had said between
bites, "there are other fish in the sea. Arnie has
lots of *other* friends. . . ."

"Spare me," Rosalie had said, starting to cry
again.

"There's someone downstairs for you, Rosalie," Mindy called again.

Who could it be? she wondered.

With her heart pounding, Rosalie flung open
the door. Barefoot, light-headed, wrapped in
her tea-stained chenille bathrobe, she plodded
down the steep flight of stairs to the reception
area.

She blinked. There, waiting for her, stood Professor Josiah Mendelsohn Bloom.

"Miss Samotsky?" he asked gently. "I've missed you in class. I hope you haven't been ill."

She didn't know what to say. It amazed her that this great, learned man had even noticed that she was absent from his class. It amazed her that he even knew her name.

He looked at her tenderly. She had the feeling that he could read her mind, her thoughts, her very soul.

He handed her a sheaf of papers. "I thought you might want these. To catch up on your reading." He paused. "I want you to know," he said softly, "that you're one of my most promising students. . . ."

Wordlessly, she took the papers. She raised her eyes and saw that Professor Bloom was studying her carefully. For the first time in days she became conscious of how she looked. "I must look . . ." she began.

"Like the Wicked Witch of the West? Nonsense!" he said. "You couldn't possibly look anything less than beautiful, Rosalie."

It was the nicest thing anyone had ever said to her. Tears came to her eyes. Before she knew it, she was sobbing uncontrollably.

She felt his arms close around her. "Shhh, shhh," he soothed, his hands smoothing her hair. "Such wild, beautiful hair . . ."

She could hear the powerful, steady beating

of his heart. She felt the strength returning to her limbs, to her heart. They stood like that for long moments. Vaguely, she began to sense that they were not alone.

When she looked up she saw that Mindy Epstein was watching from the doorway.

Mindy was smiling.

That was the beginning. She had loved Bloom for so long from afar that loving him up close took a little getting used to.

She trusted him from the beginning. The morning he had rescued her in the dorm, he'd asked her to breakfast at the Tinguely Inn, where, suddenly ravenous, she'd eaten a breakfast of scrambled eggs, hash browns, four slices of toast slathered with butter and jam, and drained three cups of coffee—light, with two sugars.

His eyes never left her.

When she was finished she sat back and smiled at him.

"Feeling better?" he asked.

She nodded. "I don't know how to . . ."

"Thank me? Don't be silly. A young woman with your ability can't allow herself to be side-tracked by an unfortunate love affair. . . ."

Rosalie felt herself blush. "So you've . . ."

"Heard about you and Sheldon? Word gets around. Windsor College is like a small town.

Someone sneezes at one end of the campus and it reverberates at the opposite end."

She thought about it. Suddenly, Sheldon Grasch seemed insignificant.

As if reading her mind, Professor Bloom said, "He's not worthy of you, Rosalie. *Rosalie,*" he repeated. "Such a fragile flower. A rose of such inner beauty needs inner nurturing. . . ."

His voice was mesmerizing. Sitting this close to him, Rosalie became aware of just how handsome Professor Bloom really was. In spite of the large nose and unruly red hair, he was so incredibly appealing. The blue eyes, reflecting his brilliance, were at once kind and knowing.

"I wonder, Rosalie," he began almost shyly, "if you would do me a supreme favor."

What could this great man possibly need from her? "Anything, Professor Bloom."

He looked at her. "Actually, *two* supreme favors. First, I need an assistant for Saturday mornings. Someone who can type, who can take shorthand. And second," he said, a tide of crimson rising to his cheeks, "please call me Bloom. . . ."

And so they had begun.

It was the best year of her life. But she knew it would have to end; he had made that plain from the start. When she graduated it would be over. . . .

* * *

The moss was a cool cushion beneath her back. The golden rays of sunlight fell obliquely upon them, warming them, bathing them in incandescence.

It was the end of May. Outside the cave the flowering bushes and trees were in full bloom. The birds were already singing their summer songs.

"I can't believe I'm never going to see this place again," Rosalie sighed.

He was inside her, his eyes closed in ecstasy. He began to move against her, slowly, teasingly, carefully stoking the fire within her. "No talk of partings, my lovely American Beauty Rose," he crooned, covering her face with kisses.

How could she ever live without him?

On the other hand, what choice did she have?

"I'll never leave Nora," he had told her at the beginning. And in the middle. And now at the end. "Nora is not a strong woman. She's not strong like you are. You're a survivor, Rosalie. Nora would perish if I left her."

Rosalie's heart broke for him. What a tragedy. He had told her the story of how he and Nora had met in Amsterdam, long ago, when he was just starting his career. How they'd lost their child before it was even born. How Nora had never been able to have another.

"How I wanted to be a father. To be a part of

the miracle of creation. . . ." A wistful sadness overtook him at such moments.

She would have done *anything* for this man.

She wasn't sure when the idea occurred to her. But once it had taken hold, it was a fait accompli. By choosing to leave her diaphragm at home, Rosalie had figured out a way to keep Bloom with her always.

She wrapped her legs around his back and clung tightly to him. "Oh, my darling, darling Bloom!" she gasped as he exploded inside of her. As orgasm overtook her seconds later, she *willed* herself to conceive.

As though reading her mind, Bloom whispered, "Don't be sad, my fragile, my perfect rose. A part of me will always be with you."

He had been right about that. . . .

Now, at the thought of Josie, Rosalie sighed. She glanced at the sleeping girl beside her in the limousine. "Bluma," she said softly. "Bluma, it's time to wake up. We're here."

Bluma rubbed her eyes and stretched sleepily. She glanced through the tinted glass window of the limo. "I didn't mean to fall asleep," she said apologetically.

Rosalie smiled. There was something so endearing about this girl, something so familiar. A certain expression. Gestures.

Henry held open the limo door while they climbed out. Rosalie shivered in her thin Valen-

tino silk dress. Bluma must be frozen in that thin
peasant blouse of hers, she thought.

"I have to call my Uncle Ernesto," Bluma said
through chattering teeth.

"Let's see. I believe there's a phone just inside
the dorm. You can call him from there," Rosalie
said.

The two women stood together in silence for a
moment, and then Bluma leaned forward to
give Rosalie a hug. "How can I ever thank you?"
Bluma said.

"It was my pleasure, dear."

Rosalie looked around. Was she really here?
After all these years? She could sense Bloom's
presence. Across the campus she could see the
outline of Hegel Hall in the darkness. Did he still
work late into the night? How she would love to
pay him a little visit. But did she dare? And if she
did dare, would she tell him about Josie? He
didn't know, of course. Not once, in any of her
letters to him, had she mentioned even a
word—

Before she could finish the thought, a tow
truck clanged to the curb. It was pulling an old,
green Dodge.

A pretty dark-haired woman climbed down
from the cab. "So it'll be ready by tomorrow
afternoon?" she was asking the driver nervously.

"No problem, lady," the driver replied as he

pulled noisily away. The Dodge bounced crazily behind the truck.

The dark-haired woman winced. "Damn. It's my brother's car. If anything happens to it, I'll owe him my life."

For the first time she seemed to notice Rosalie standing there. They smiled at each other. Did Rosalie know her? She did look slightly familiar.

But then, she was a Windsor girl, wasn't she?

CHAPTER NINE

Nora

They'd been coming now for hours—*his girls*. His eternal, infernal, nocturnal girls.

They arrived in an endless stream. By car. By taxi. By bus, Even, now, by limousine.

She stood by the window and peered through the binoculars. Two of them were getting out of the limousine. A mother and daughter act? No. Even at this distance, even in the dark, she could see that these two were not related. One looked foreign, with long, unkempt hair and cheap clothing. The other was more his type: good clothes, good body, that same look of anticipatory rapture she'd seen on all their faces.

She set down the binoculars. Her head was beginning to throb. She reached into her pocket and withdrew two pills—a yellow and a blue—from her own private rainbow of comfort. She swallowed them with the last of the vodka. After a moment the throbbing eased.

She squinted through the window once more. Would she be able to go through with her plan?

Of course she would. She'd gotten this far, hadn't she?

CHAPTER TEN

Daphne

She'd been driving how long? Twelve hours. It seemed like a lifetime. Normally it was a three-hour trip from New York to Tinguely. What was it with Sid's car? No matter how much she accelerated, it refused to go more than forty miles per hour. It would be just like Sid to have had his mechanic fiddle with it to get better mileage.

But, on the other hand, maybe that's what Rovers did. They roved. Well, that might be okay for the Queen of England when she was tooling around Windsor Castle, but it wasn't okay for Daphne Andrews Banks en route to Windsor College!

The frustrated shouts of the other drivers still rang in her ears: "Get a horse, lady!" "Get a *real* car, bimbo!"

Somewhere between Bridgeport and New Haven, a state trooper had ordered her off the highway. "Lady, speed up or get off the big road!" he'd commanded. But the Rover stubbornly refused to speed up, and so she was banished to the back roads. Where she promptly got lost.

Now, at last, she was approaching the campus. With a sigh, she turned down East Windsor Avenue past the stately faculty homes with their ivy-covered brick facades. Daphne felt a tingle in her spine. She was so close to him! Again she wondered if Bloom had seen her in the Scrumptious commercials. Had he seen the ads? What would he think? Would he be proud of her achievement in the popular media or would he think she'd sold out to crass commercialism?

She made a right turn onto Campus Drive. The invitation had said to park behind Elias Windsor Hall and Dining Facility, but she could see that all the spaces were filled. She must be the last to arrive. Trembling with fatigue, she made a U-turn and headed west. She knew there was a small parking lot behind Hegel Hall. . . .

The bright red MG-B, Daddy's birthday present to her, refused to start. She pumped the gas pedal again and turned the key, and still nothing. *"Shitsky!"* she muttered, and got out of the car to peer under the hood.

Not that she had any idea what was under there. All those tubes and pipes were as mysterious to her as the formulas in the quantum physics course she'd barely passed last year.

She wished Freddie were here. He knew everything there was to know about cars. But Freddie was a hundred miles away in New Haven, waiting for her right this minute!

She straightened and squinted into the late afternoon sun. At four o'clock on a Friday afternoon the campus was all but deserted. All the girls were either in the dorms getting ready for dates, on their way home, or en route to meet their boyfriends. Except, of course, for those few pathetic grinds over in Egmont Hall, who were probably studying for a quiz next Wednesday.

She turned and looked at the Gothic stone facade of Hegel Hall. The gargoyles were leering at her. She made a face back at them and then fished in her pocket for a dime. There was a pay phone just inside Hegel Hall. But she hesitated. Did she really want to go back in there and risk bumping into Professor Bloom again?

The conference had been embarrassing enough.

"You have a keen, perceptive mind, Miss Andrews," he'd said only moments ago. "If this were anyone else's paper, I'd give it an *A* immediately. But I know you're capable of much more, so I'm asking you to do it over."

Unlike other professors who'd chalked her up as an airhead, Professor Bloom seemed to see right through her. He was right about the paper on Kant's *Critique of Pure Reason*. She'd tossed it off in less than twenty minutes last night—after a stimulating telephone fuck with Freddie.

> Freddie: "I'd like to ease my engine right into your garage."
> Daphne: (Giggling) "Well, Freddykins, the garage door's wide open. . . ."

It was a miracle she'd gotten the paper done at all.

"I can't do Kant," she'd said to Professor Bloom.

"I wish you wouldn't do that, Miss Andrews. Such flippancy doesn't suit you."

She had bristled. She looked at him. Up close like this, Professor Bloom was so much better-looking than she'd thought. There was something about his eyes, the way they looked at you and really *saw* into you. Under that tacky tweed jacket of his, there seemed to be a real body, an athlete's body. How old *was* he, anyway?

He cleared his throat. "Listen here, Miss Andrews—"

"Please," she interrupted. "Call me . . ."

"Daphne?" The blue eyes had sparkled. "Daphne, I repeat. You have tremendous potential. You have the ability to grasp very difficult abstract concepts. . . ."

His voice was magnetic. What he was saying was true. She *was* capable of much better. She'd always known that she was smarter than the other girls. But early on she'd learned to disguise her intelligence, to blend in. To be not so smart. As she had gotten older it had become clear to her that smarts were a no-no. Guys were so easily intimidated. Looks, on the other hand, turned them on. It was as simple as that.

"I'll try harder, Professor Bloom. I really will."

He had smiled. Daphne didn't think he'd been convinced.

And now this car business! She looked at her watch. *Four-fifteen.* Freddie hated it when she made him wait. "Get your bod down here in a hurry," he'd half-kidded on the phone last night. "Bring your toothbrush."

Her toothbrush and her nightie—a black lace number with peekaboo bodice—were in the overnight bag in the car. Should she call the Auto Club? Should she call a taxi? Should she call Freddie? Whatever she did, she had to call somebody.

She and Professor Bloom collided on the steps of Hegel Hall. He looked surprised. "Miss Andrews, I'd have thought you'd be long gone by now," he said.

"It's Daphne," she reminded him. She felt her cheeks flush. The man was *definitely* attractive. "My car died," she said. "I've got to make a telephone call."

He peered beyond her at the MG-B that was

audaciously parked in a faculty spot. "That's too bad," he said. "Would you like to use the phone in my office?"

Daphne hesitated. "That's okay. I can use the . . ."

"Public phone?" He shook his head. "It's out of order," he said.

She shrugged. The matter was decided for her.

And so it had begun. The love affair to end all love affairs.

She'd called the Auto Club and was told someone would be there in forty-five minutes to an hour. Professor Bloom offered her some tea while she waited. They'd sat on his leather sofa and talked philosophy. And talked and talked. How easy it was to express herself to him. To verbalize her insights on Life and Love and Truth and Beauty. For here, in his sanctum sanctorum, she felt freed from the constraints of social judgment. In other words, she could be herself.

It all happened so quickly.

It was so natural. One moment she was talking about the implications of Good in an Evil world, and the next moment his tongue was in her mouth and his hand was on her breast.

Time had ceased to exist. Evening blended into night, night into dawn, and they were One. This was no mere boy seeking his own pleasure.

This was no callous youth who took without giving.

Instead, she sensed that Bloom was a man who had known tragedy and loss and who had learned the true meaning of love. He was tender. He was patient. He was kind.

He was ever the teacher.

"Ease your tongue along the base very lightly," he'd suggested as she eagerly buried her face between his thighs. She had been right about his body. He was strong and muscular. But his hands were sensitive as they positioned her.

"Now, slowly, as you reach the tip, increase the pressure. *Lips*, Daphne, my beautiful daffodil, *lips*. Lips and tongue. Yes . . . that's it! What a mind! Circular motions . . . yes . . . ahhhhh!"

Such control! So unlike Freddie. Bloom was on the verge of coming, but he saved it until he entered her. At once, they came together. A second time. A third.

"My golden daffodil," he'd whispered hotly against her neck as he inserted his splendid tool into her yet again. "You are the most fragrant flower in the garden of earthly delights."

She never did find out if the Auto Club came or not.

She almost lost Freddie that weekend. While it was Bloom she loved, it was Freddie she needed. There was no doubt about it. She absolutely *needed* Freddie Banks to get her through her senior year. Who would escort her to the Yale-Harvard Game? The Holiday Ball at Windsor? The Christmas Frolic?

Bloom, she knew, was trapped by both position and destiny. He'd made it clear from the start that he would never leave that cold fish of a wife of his, Nora Haddock Bloom.

Late Saturday afternoon, when she finally returned to her sorority house, she found a stack of messages as high as Mount Everest.

"Somebody wants to know where you've been all night," taunted Muffy Tyler, who, Daphne knew, had the hots for Freddie.

"Car trouble," Daphne said hurriedly as she rushed to make the conciliatory phone call.

"Yeah. Right," sneered Muffy. "Backseat or front seat?"

As she expected, Freddie was fit to be tied. "Where the hell *were* you?" he screamed. "I waited for you till my balls turned blue!"

She had her alibi all planned. Calmly, she explained that the car wouldn't start. "I called the Auto Club and I waited three hours and they never came. . . ."

"So why didn't you call me?" Freddie wanted to know.

"I did! But you never answered!" She broke into tears.

His voice softened. "What number did you call?"

"Your dorm number," she said innocently, "4 - 2 - 6 - 8."

"Daphne!" he exploded. "It's 4 - 2 - 5 - 8!"

"Shitsky!" she said, still in tears. "You *know* I'm lousy with numbers. You *know* that. . . ."

He knew that. Or he thought he did. And he forgave her, as she knew he would.

The Hegel Hall parking lot was indeed empty, just as she'd thought. In the dark, with only the streetlights for illumination, the building seemed unchanged. How she ached to see him. Not a day had passed that she hadn't thought of him. How often she'd been tempted to send him a photo of Josh, their son, the son he'd so desperately wanted. But how could she have? It would serve no purpose. "I'll never leave Nora" was a refrain that ran through the fabric of her life like a warped thread.

Daphne sighed and reached into the Land Rover for her suitcase. Well, at least she was here. At least she would see him tomorrow night at the farewell banquet.

Could she last that long?

CHAPTER ELEVEN

Bloom

Was it his fault he'd always been able to understand everything right away?

It was both a blessing and a curse.

As an infant he'd been able to fathom every
word his parents burbled at him. Before he was
able to speak, he could think. Frustrating as hell,
but there it was.

As a kid growing up in Brooklyn, things only
got worse. Enslaved in the public school system,
which was no more than a baby-sitting service,
he always knew beforehand what his teachers
were about to say. Without meaning to he'd begun to finish their sentences for them—which
was, understandably, irritating for them. Perhaps that explained in part why they skipped
him so often: from first grade to third, from third
to fifth, then from fifth into high school. By the
time he was thirteen he'd won a full scholarship

to Princeton University and a place directly under Einstein at the Institute for Advanced Studies.

And then one day the inevitable happened.

Einstein, in wrinkled lab coat, white hair shooting every which way, had begun yet another lecture on the unified theory. "Zo, ziss vill proof zat zere rrrreally iss . . ."

Automatically, fifteen-year-old Bloom finished the thought: ". . . ze pozzibility zat zound und ze light equvals ze grrrreatest forze in ze univerze. . . ."

Einstein glared at him. "Shaddup already! *I'm* talking, you shmardy-pents!"

That very afternoon young Bloom had been advised by the dean that perhaps it might be best if he decided to give physics a go-by. Would he like to try philosophy?

And thus had begun the long love affair with philosophical thought.

From time to time through the years he'd dabbled in other disciplines—botany, linguistics, literature, biochemistry, etc.—but he always came back to his old buddies: Aristotle, Plato, Hegel, Kant, Buscaglia, et al.

Now he looked around his office and sighed. His beloved office. After thirty-five years it wasn't going to be easy to leave it.

Absently, he resumed packing. How he hated to put his life into corrugated cartons. The walls were already beginning to take on that barren look. *Barren.* Immediately his mind jumped to thoughts of Nora. Nora, his eternal torment.

Wearily, he sank down into his well-worn leather chair. The springs creaked reassuringly. Strange how one derived comfort from small things. He reached into his pocket and found the key. Slowly he inserted it into the lock and opened the lower right-hand desk drawer.

He looked at the stack of unopened letters. Daisy's were on the top of the pile, still fresh and untouched by time. Ah, Daisy Gabboulian. She'd offered to stay and help him pack, but of course he'd declined.

"No, my fragile Daisy, my beautiful, perfect flower. It's better that we say farewell now. A part of me will forever be with you . . ." he'd said, kissing her tears away. Only two weeks had passed since graduation, but already she'd written him three letters. There would be more, he knew. He also knew that, in time, she would stop writing to him. She would get on with her life as if he never existed. Which was, he thought, as it should be.

Behind the letters was the small teak box that Iris Ledbetter had given him at the end of his first year at Windsor. He opened it. His *memory* box. Tangible evidence that his bouquet, his beloved flowers, were—how to say it? Were? He shrugged. More than memories. Proof that he *had* loved, that he *could* love, that he would never stop loving.

Idly, he riffled through the cards, some of them yellowed and bent with age. Loomis, Petunia, '62 (Sept. 3). Trubenik, Violet, '59 (May 6). O'Neill, Chrysanthemum, '74 (Dec. 15). Ledbetter, Iris, '53 (Aug. 2). Daisy's bright new card appeared: Gabboulian, Daisy, '88 (March 12).

He snapped the little teak box shut and put it hastily back into the drawer. He wasn't up to packing it just yet. What time was it, anyway? A glance at his watch told him it was close to eleven. He would have to get back to the house. Back to Nora. He sighed wearily. He reached into his pocket for an antacid tablet.

It was always back to Nora. Would it never end?

He'd met her at a café in Amsterdam the summer he was working on the tulip project with Van Bergen. He was nineteen. His whole life was in front of him. . . .

There she sat, the sun making a halo of her wild, black hair. For a heart-stopping moment he thought he'd found his Estrella at last. Even her smile was perfectly imperfect, just like Estrella's. He stared at her a moment too long. It was the worst mistake of his life.

She beckoned to him. She bought him a drink. He was surprised to discover she was an American, spending the summer here in Amsterdam at the ZuDreitn Haus. He'd thought it was a hotel. How was he to know it was a sanitarium for the insane rich?

They'd spent the rest of the afternoon strolling hand in hand along the canal, and the entire night fucking in his cramped room above Van Bergen's lab. It was only the second time he'd been with a woman, but he hadn't forgotten a thing. Estrella had taught him well.

Nora was insatiable. She was twenty-four, older than he, and more experienced. She was also pretty, and it wasn't long before he convinced himself that he was in love with her.

Part of it was that he was flattered. After all, he was only a skinny kid with carrot-red hair and a big nose and no money to speak of.

Nora came from Yankee stock. Her father, Philmont Haddock, was president of Windsor College. Bloom was impressed. Naturally, he'd heard of Windsor. In fact, Van Bergen had been a visiting professor there just the year before.

Before the week was out, they were married.

The ceremony, such as it was, took place on a houseboat on the canal at high noon. White clouds dotted the Dutch sky above. Nora looked fetching in a gauzy purple dress. She carried a bouquet of rare black orchids. The wind blew her dark hair wildly about her head.

Before the ceremony Van Bergen took him aside. "Are you absolutely certain *this* is the woman you wish to marry?" The botanist looked concerned.

Bloom nodded. The truth was, he wasn't *absolutely* certain. But then there were no absolute certainties in life. Besides, he had already lost *one* love. How could he take the chance of losing another?

Bloom clicked off his desk lamp. All that was so long ago. He had been such a young fool. What would his life have been like without Nora? The prospect was so overwhelming, he could not bear to contemplate it. . . .

He heard a car door slam. Who could be parking in the Hegel Hall lot at this time of night? In the darkness he got up and walked over to the window. He saw someone walking away from a squarish vehicle. She was carrying a suitcase, whoever she was. Probably a summer-school student. But wasn't it a bit early for that?

He felt a nagging pain in his left arm. He flexed it. Must be from all the packing. He looked across the campus. It was a clear night. He could see the outline of Andrews Chapel against the starry sky. Farther to the left, the long, low silhouette of Elias Windsor Hall and Dining Facility glowed with light. Something was going on.

He shrugged. Well, whatever it was, it didn't concern him. Nothing at Windsor College concerned him any longer. By next week he would be peering out of a different window. A window in Washington, D.C. A window overlooking a rose garden.

CHAPTER TWELVE

Breakfast

Chrystal looked around. Elias Windsor Hall's Dining Facility was as tired and worn out as she was. Faded flowered draperies hung limp at the windows. The windows themselves looked as if they hadn't been washed since her graduation fourteen years before.

Where *was* everybody? She had assumed there would be hundreds of Bloom's former students here to wish him a fond farewell. Oh well, maybe they weren't staying in the dorm. Maybe they were staying at the Royal Windsor Motel on Route 2. Smart. The beds here were worse than ever. She hadn't been able to sleep a wink all night. Of course the beds weren't entirely to blame.

For one thing, she was on edge. There had been the long drive. Then the flat. Then the worry about Sean's Dodge. But those were only superficial reasons. The *real* reason she hadn't slept, she knew, had to do with something much more primal: *Bloom* . . .

Someone bumped into her. She turned.

"Oops. Sorry," said Rosalie Fineberg, her roommate for the weekend. "I'm not functioning too well this morning."

"Join the club," Chrystal said, handing Rosalie a tray. "We both had a hard night."

Slowly they shuffled through the line. The girl behind the coffee urn—the dark-eyed beauty with the unruly hair who'd come in the limo with Rosalie last night—gave them a smile of recognition.

"Good morning, ladies." she said, filling their cups. "How are you this morning?"

"I've been better," Rosalie said.

Ditto, thought Chrystal as she found a table near the windows.

Chrystal took a sip of the coffee and made a face. This wasn't coffee! This was water tinted brown! Whoever made this wouldn't last two minutes at the Harbor View All-Night Diner!

Rosalie sat down beside her.

"Watch out for the coffee," Chrystal advised. "It's a little on the weak side."

Rosalie took a sip. Her eyes widened and she put the cup down. "Poor Bluma," she said. "It's her first day. She's probably nervous."

"Where do you know her from, Rosalie?"

"She was stranded at the airport last night. I gave her a ride. A sweet kid . . ."

Chrystal smiled. "So. She's a work-study." She paused. "So was I."

Rosalie looked at her. "I had a job too," she said. "Saturday mornings. My senior year."

Chrystal nodded. "Me, too," she said, remembering her mornings with Bloom. She was about to say more, but decided not to. Instead, she sighed.

They lapsed into silence. She looked at the food she had chosen: grapefruit sections, eggs. She should eat. But she wasn't hungry. Who could eat when the only man she'd ever loved was so close she could almost touch him?

"Hi, girls. Mind if I join you?"

Chrystal looked up. Even Daphne Banks, one of the most truly beautiful women she'd ever seen, looked drawn and tired in the thin, pale sunlight that filtered through the begrimed windows.

"Did you get any sleep at all last night?" Rosalie asked.

Daphne shrugged. "Not much."

The woman really was gorgeous. Chrystal couldn't take her eyes off her. Tall and slender, her skin almost poreless, she looked as if she'd just stepped out of the pages of a magazine. Which, Chrystal realized with a start, she *had*! My God—Daphne is the Scrumptious Yogurt Girl! Chrystal thought.

Half the women in the Dining Facility had stopped eating and were staring at Daphne. Only Rosalie seemed unfazed that they had a celebrity in their midst.

Daphne took a sip of her coffee and went "Blah-h-h!"

Rosalie and Chrystal laughed.

"It's no joke," Daphne said. "I need my coffee in the morning! What *is* this brew?"

"It's not much worse than it used to be," Rosalie said. "At least when I was here. . . ."

Daphne was busily adding sugar.

Chrystal wondered how she could consume six cubes of sugar and still look fantastic. "How do you do it?" she said. "How do you stay so gorgeous?"

Daphne sighed and shook her head. "Chrystal, please, don't hold it against me. I didn't ask to look like this. . . ."

Chrystal smiled. Daphne was all right. So was Rosalie. But she wasn't so sure about Iris Ledbetter, who was bearing down on their table right this minute, carrying a tray laden with Danish and hard rolls.

"So whaddya say, Scrumptious?" Iris blurted. She took a seat beside Daphne and raised a glass of watery orange juice: "To the living legend! Josiah Mendelsohn Bloom! Long may he reign!" She downed the juice in a single gulp.

Chrystal repeated the toast silently. God bless the father of my Jace, she thought, taking a sip of the adulterated juice. She hoped the conversation would veer away from Bloom. Although they were here today because of him, she felt uncomfortable talking about him with them.

Evidently, Rosalie felt the same way because she changed the subject immediately. "It's a gorgeous day, isn't it?"

Chrystal let the conversation flow around her. First they talked about the weather. Then hemlines. Then, inevitably, husbands. Iris had had four. Daphne had none at present. Rosalie had one.

Chrystal thought of Vinnie. Last night when she'd called he'd answered the phone right away. He sounded unusually alert for such a late hour. And genuinely pleased to hear from her.

"So how're things up there?" he'd asked.

"I just got here, Vin," she'd sighed. She told him about the flat. She expected him to get angry at her. Somehow, with Vinnie, everything was always her fault.

Instead, Vinnie said, "Don't worry about it, honey. Everything'll be okay."

Why was Vinnie being so nice to her? Could he possibly have figured out the real reason she'd come to Windsor this weekend? Could he possibly know about her love for Bloom, which hadn't diminished one iota with the passing years? "Are the kids okay?" she'd asked quickly, changing the subject.

"The girls are all asleep."

"And Jace?"

There was silence. "He's up in his room," Vinnie said after a moment. "He's working on one of his projects. Jeez-us, Chrystal! It's Friday night, for God's sake! He can't even let up and watch the ballgame!"

Poor Vinnie, Chrystal thought. He was eternally perplexed when it came to Jace. He couldn't understand him, and he never would. But then, who could expect him to?

Her mother had been the first to notice.

It was early summer. She'd been home from Windsor six whole weeks and still hadn't found a job. The truth was, she didn't want a job. She wanted to be a writer.

"I heard you being sick in the bathroom again this morning, Chrys," her mother said, pouring her a second cup of tea.

Chrystal lifted the cup with both hands. She said nothing. In the summer her mother moved the dryers and manicuring table out onto the porch, but the permanents were still done at the kitchen sink. The acrid smell of chemicals was making her sick all over again.

Her mother clicked her tongue. "Who is he?" she asked matter-of-factly.

Chrystal pretended not to understand the question. "It's a virus, that's all," she said quietly.

Her mother slammed the kettle down on the stove. "A virus me eye!" she said. Whenever her mother got angry, her Irish brogue intensified. "So that's what they're callin' it nowadays! Who's the man?" her mother asked again.

How could Chrystal begin to explain? How she, Chrystal O'Neill from Boonton Harbor, New Jersey, had been chosen by fate to carry the seed of one of the greatest thinkers in the history of the world?

Her mother was glaring at her. "It's nothing to smile about, my dear girl!"

The doctor confirmed what she already knew. "You're better than two months down the pike," he said stealing a glance at her ringless finger. He asked somberly, "Have you considered the alternatives?"

She had considered the alternatives and dismissed them. Abortion was out of the question, naturally. So was giving up the baby for adoption. She would die before she'd give up Bloom's baby—the baby he'd yearned for all his life. The baby his wife could never give him.

No, she would keep this baby. Keep it and cherish it. Love it and bring it up to be a fine human being.

She could never have Bloom. She knew that . . . and accepted it. But she could have the next best thing.

* * *

"Vinnie Malatesta is a perfectly presentable young man," her mother argued. "Even your poor dead father would have approved. And the man is crazy about you!"

Chrystal wiped her eyes. They were ganging up on her. Her mother, her brother Sean, her father's sister Meagan and Meagan's daughter Fiona, who was nine months pregnant with her sixth. They were all sitting around the dining-room table, pinning her with their eyes.

"There's no way she's going to disgrace my brother's good name and bear a little bastard!" screamed Aunt Meagan.

Fiona, cracking her gum, said, "I think Vinnie's kinda cute, Chrys, even if he *is* Eye-talian. I always dug dago guys myself. . . ."

Her brother Sean took his turn. "Vinnie's a good guy, Chrys. He'll put a damn good roof over your head."

Chrystal looked up at him. "Sure he will, Sean," she cracked. "He's a *roofer*!"

Her mother shook her finger at her. "There's nothing wrong with good, honest hard work, young lady!" Her mother beat her chest. "Oh, God! Why did I ever let her go to that fancy college where they filled her head with nonsense and her belly with—" She burst into tears.

Soon all the women were crying.

Chrystal, in resignation.

Her mother, in silent shame.

Aunt Meagan, in misplaced outrage.

And Fiona, bloated and fecund, in mourning at the age of twenty-eight for all the dark-haired, handsome Eye-talian men she would never know.

She'd known Vinnie Malatesta forever, it seemed. They'd been confirmed together at St. Agnes's. They'd had their knuckles rapped by Sister Ignatia in sixth grade. Later they'd dated off and on, had experienced their first pantings and gropings in the backseat of Vinnie's old Ford.

But never, not once, had Chrystal ever imagined marrying Vinnie Malatesta. Not once, during her four years at Windsor, had she answered his letters. Summers, when he'd come around begging her to go to the movies with him, she always managed to have something else to do.

They were married in St. Agnes's on a rainy Saturday afternoon with old Father Ryan officiating. They spent their honeymoon in a heart-shaped bed at the Valley View Lodge in the Poconos, where, as far as Vinnie was concerned, their first child was conceived.

Iris Ledbetter was nattering on about her multiple marriages.

"I wasn't going to take that crap from any

man! Imagine . . . the sonofabitch was fucking his blond bimbo of a secretary while I was at consciousness-raising! In my own bed, yet!" She paused meaningfully. "So naturally I cut all the buttons off his shirts."

Rosalie squirmed. She hated it when women she hardly knew spilled out the most intimate details of their lives. But if her husband had been fucking his secretary, maybe Iris was justified in doing something so drastic. She tried the coffee again; she could hardly swallow the stuff.

If only she wasn't so tired. But who could sleep with that Iris Ledbetter snoring like a buzz saw in the next room? No wonder poor Daphne had been driven, pillow in hand at 3 A.M., to bunk on their floor.

"And my fourth husband wasn't much better," Iris was saying. "I can't begin to tell you what that debauched bastard made me do to him. . . ."

Rosalie was sure, however, that Iris *would* begin to tell them. And so she tuned out. If only she could find a polite way of excusing herself. *Where was he?* Hegel Hall? Jogging around the campus? Her heart ached with longing for him, her Bloom. She sighed.

Discreetly, she looked at the other women. Next to her, Chrystal sat with a glazed expression, obviously as bored listening to Iris Ledbetter as she, herself, was. Even Daphne looked ready to scream. Still, even without a good

night's sleep, Daphne didn't look the worse for
wear. Rosalie had seen those yogurt commercials of course. But Daphne was even lovelier in
person. With the right lighting and a good cinematographer—someone like Antonio Imbroglioni—she was certain that Daphne Banks
could make it big in Hollywood.

Should she call Kermit and tell him she'd
found his next big star? She considered for a
moment. God only knew what Kermit was up to
at this very moment. Maybe, like Iris's ex-husband, he was fucking some dumb bimbo in *her*
very own bed. . . .

She looked around. The dining room was
nearly empty. She was surprised that so few of
Bloom's former students were here for his farewell dinner. She had assumed that hundreds,
maybe even thousands, of them would be invited.

Well, it was still early. Maybe by tonight . . .

Tonight. It was only 10 A.M. The cocktail party
was at six. Could she wait that long to see him
again?

It seemed she had been waiting her whole life
to see Bloom again. But what would she say
when she saw him? Could she tell him that he
had a daughter who looked just like him? Or,
rather, *used to* look just like him? Josie was such
a wonderful, brilliant child. He would be so
proud. But no, she *couldn't* tell him about Josie.
She had made a pact with herself never to in-

trude on his life. Because, in the end, what good would it do if he knew about Josie? He had committed himself to that bête noire of his, that Nora, that cold fish of a wife. Any man less noble would have left that woman long ago. But not Bloom. And she loved him all the more for it. . . .

Her eyes felt like sandpaper. She fished in her purse for a tissue. If she cried now, how could she explain it to the other women? She blew her nose and looked up. The sun was shining weakly through the grimy windows. . . .

The motel-room window was so filthy she could barely see through it. Which, when she thought about it later, was probably no accident. The doctor glowered at her as he snapped on his rubber gloves. "Get away from the window," he commanded in a harsh voice.

"And keep quiet, Rosalie. We can't make any noise."

Wordlessly, she nodded. She had never felt so helpless in her life. She didn't want to be here, but her mother had made it clear that she had no choice.

"For a smart girl, ya ain't got no brains, Rosalie!" her mother had screamed when she discovered Rosalie's secret. "Don't you know to take precautions? How could you be so dumb?"

Her father was on the verge of collapse. *"Oy! Vey!* What I did to deserve such *tsouris?"* He paced in circles, stopping now and then to rend his garments.

"Max, Max, sha! Your blood pressure . . ." her mother mollified. To Rosalie she said, "I hope he was a Jewish boy at least."

They went on and on like that for days until Rosalie was willing to do anything they asked.

She took the yellow pills her mother gave her. She jumped up and down at least a hundred times a day. She took baths as hot as she could stand, and then she took cold showers. Everything she did was "guaranteed" to bring on her period. When nothing worked she felt a small satisfaction.

At the end of the week her father was ready to drape the mirrors with black crepe and sit shiva for her. But her mother had one more trick up her sleeve. "My friend Frieda's nephew, the doctor, must know someone. . . ."

Frieda's nephew-the-doctor did, indeed, know someone. He was tall and gaunt and wore a white mask to hide the lower part of his face. His eyes were hidden behind thick lenses, but Rosalie suspected that however myopic those eyes were, they were, nevertheless, cold and unfeeling.

He asked for his fee—$750—the minute she entered the motel room.

She put the money on the dresser.

"Take off your skirt and underpants and get on the bed."

She moved as though in a trance. From far away she heard the hum of traffic on the highway. Outside in the parking lot, her mother and Frieda waited in Frieda's husband's Mercury.

She didn't want to do this thing. She already loved the seedling that was growing so innocently inside her. She knew other girls who had had abortions. They were sad, lonely girls who hadn't *wanted* to get pregnant. *That was the difference.* She *had* wanted to get pregnant. The only trouble was, she hadn't thought it through. Maybe it was selfish of her. Maybe even stupid. Because in 1971 being an unwed mother wasn't easy.

But she loved Bloom. How could she destroy his seed?

"Rosalie, come on!" the doctor hissed nervously. "Put your knees up and spread them!"

She couldn't move. It irked her that he knew her name and she didn't know his.

"Look, missy, I don't have all day! It's now or never!"

When she didn't do as he told her, an angry flush crept over the top half of his face. "Rosalie!" he screamed. "Do you want this abortion or not?"

It took her only a moment to answer. *"Not!"* she shouted, hurling herself off the bed. *"Not!*

Not!" she screamed again, grabbing the $750 off
the dresser before he could stop her.

"You're out of your mind!" he screamed as she
fled out into the warm Bakersfield sun.

The $750 got her to Los Angeles. On her first
day there she found a small furnished studio
apartment off Doheny. It would do until the
baby was born, sometime around Valentine's
Day.

On her second day in town she landed a job in
the typing pool at Fineberg Films.

"I hope you're not one of those girls with 'aspi-
rations,' Miss Samotsky," warned the stony-
faced office manager, Miss Beamish. "This job is
strictly typing. Period. You catch my drift?"

Rosalie caught her drift. But she didn't care.
The job would cover her expenses if she was
careful. She might even be able to put away a
couple of dollars a week so she wouldn't have to
work immediately after the baby came.

But she would worry about that later.

And so she typed. Day after day. Script after
lousy script, each one more derivative than the
last: *Boat of Clowns; Ecstasy on the Lawn; Kitty
on a Cool Tile Floor.* Just to keep herself awake
as she typed, she began to add a word here and
there. Soon she grew bolder and started adding
sentences. After three months on the job, she
threw caution to the winds and began to rewrite
whole paragraphs.

* * *

"The senior Mr. Fineberg would like to see you in his office immediately!" Miss Beamish barked nastily one morning.

Uh-oh, thought Rosalie. The shit was about to hit. Dry-mouthed and queasy, she entered the glitzy private office of Kermit O. Fineberg. She'd seen him on several occasions, always from afar, getting into and out of his long, black limousine. Up close he looked younger, however. His longish brown hair fell nearly to his shoulders. His face was ruddy, round, and deeply tanned. Rosalie found herself wondering about him. He had three sons, all of them grown. He had been divorced twice, according to the office gossip. He was somewhere in his forties, she guessed. Seated behind his massive desk, he was also intimidating.

He didn't bother to look up as she entered. She sat down without waiting for him to acknowledge her. If he was going to fire her, well, let him, she thought. There were other typing pools in town.

Moments passed and still he didn't look up. So she took the bull by the horns and asked, "Do you ignore all your employees like this?"

He looked up in surprise. His gaze was clear and direct. She was amazed to see him blushing. He cleared his throat. "I'm sorry," he said. "I didn't hear you come in."

She believed him. His desk was piled high

with scripts, some of them typed by her. He
reached into the middle of a pile, retrieved one,
and pushed it over to her side of the desk. "Miss
Samotsky, can you explain this?" he asked, tap-
ping it with his manicured forefinger.

She glanced at the script. "*Oregano's Seed*?"
she asked, trying not to laugh. With a straight
face, she said, "I believe that one's about a De-
troit housewife who gets pregnant by her demon parakeet."

There was a silence. He clapped his hand to
his forehead. "Jesus," he muttered under his
breath. And then he laughed and said, "Miss
Samotsky, I understand you fiddled with the dia-
logue. . . ."

Her heart pounded. Here it comes, she
thought. Well, let it come. "Yes, I did," she admitted. Then she added, "It won't happen
again."

He shook his head. "That's too bad," he said,
"because this script needed all the help it could
get." With two fingers he picked it up and
dropped it unceremoniously into the wastebasket.

She watched him wide-eyed. "May I ask why
Fineberg Films bought that script in the first
place?"

He cleared his throat. "Ah, the $64,000 ques-
tion! What can I tell you? Truth is, my son Marty
graduated from USC film school and brought it
in. 'It has potential,' he says to me. Me, I never

went to college, so what do I know. No wonder I'm going broke!" Kermit O. Fineberg said, throwing up his hands.

What should she do? Should she commiserate with him? Should she just sit here and say nothing?

He leaned back in his chair. His eyes swept over her rounding belly, her ringless finger, and then back to her face. He knew her story. She knew he knew it.

"USC's a good school," she finally said.

He nodded and shuffled some papers on his desk. From somewhere he pulled out a file. "I see here that you went to Windsor College." He looked up. "Now *that* is a good school."

Rosalie shrugged modestly.

"My niece Melody tried to get into Windsor. But even her father's big bucks couldn't open the door." He smiled at her. "You must be very smart."

Smart? Oh sure, she thought. *Very* smart. Five months pregnant by a man I can't marry. A man who doesn't even know I'm carrying his child.

Suddenly the reality of the situation became overwhelming. What had she done? She was about to bring a new life into the world. How was she going to provide for it?

Kermit was still looking at her file. "You double-majored in literature and philosophy?"

When she didn't answer he looked up. She

didn't want him to see her crying, so she turned her head.

"Miss Samotsky?"

When she still didn't answer he came over to her. "Here," he said, handing her a handkerchief monogrammed KOF. "Now blow."

She blew.

He knelt beside her chair and waited for her sobs to abate. From time to time he smoothed her hair with his big hand. "C'mon," he said. "Let's have a little smile. Such a smart girl. Gutsy, too. I like that in a br—in a woman." He buzzed the intercom on his desk. "Beamish. Two coffees. How do you take yours, Rosalie?"

In a small voice she said, "I'd rather have a glass of milk, if you don't mind."

"Beamish, make that one coffee and one milk."

Rosalie smiled tentatively at him. He smiled back.

They were married in the gazebo behind Kermit's K-shaped pool. The warm February sun shone beneficently on the wedding party.

Her mother wept tears of joy as Kermit smashed the glass with his foot, signifying their oneness with their ancestors. Her father, grinning from ear to ear, went around knocking on wood.

Marty, Kermit's son, the script maven, wasn't quite as joyous. Rosalie figured that was due to his demotion. As of last week Marty Fineberg had become her assistant. From now on Rosalie Samotsky Fineberg would have final say on all the scripts that came in.

Kermit was a good man. He loved her, and he promised to love her baby.

It was a promise he would keep, she knew.

Would the woman *never* shut up? Daphne wondered. Who cared that Iris Ledbetter's son had received a "genius grant" to study the gravitational pull of igneous rocks?

"He was from *which* husband?" Chrystal asked in confusion, trying to be polite.

For the first time in nearly an hour Iris fell silent. A faint blush colored her cheeks. "Uh . . . um . . . say, listen," she said, changing the subject. "Have you noticed there are only a few of us here? I mean, what kind of a reunion is this? I expected to run into half my class." She looked around. "But then, I guess, this isn't really a *reunion* reunion, is it?"

There were murmurs around the table. Daphne had been wondering why there were so few of them. It seemed odd indeed that more students hadn't come to bid farewell to Bloom. After all, it wasn't every philosopher who was chosen to serve the President of the United States.

"This place isn't going to be the same without him," Daphne said sadly.

"Well, he's really too big for Windsor," Iris posited. "The world needs him now."

I need him too, Daphne thought but didn't say.

"He's going to work wonders for the world, just you wait and see," said Rosalie.

They were silent for a moment. And then Chrystal said, "There'll probably be no more wars."

Daphne pondered that. She would love a cup of *real* coffee right now. She was tempted to ask Chrystal and Rosalie if they'd like to run over to the Tinguely Inn with her for a cup. She glanced at her watch. Ten forty-five. No time.

There was that damn bus tour of the campus at eleven. As if they needed a tour! Whose idea was it to structure every minute of their stay here? After the bus trip there was the luncheon at the Tinguely Inn. After *that* there was a tea in the new library.

God, if she could only break away, even for an hour, she could head on over to Bush Hill, where he liked to run. Maybe she'd get lucky. . . .

"You're lucky we can take care of this mess for you," her mother said imperiously. "After the abortion you'll come with us to Bear Island. Maine is the perfect place to get your mind off things."

The last thing Daphne wanted to do was get her mind off things. What she needed was to keep her mind *on* things, to think things through, possibly for the first time in her life.

Her father, seated in his favorite leather chair, held a glass of scotch in his hand. Lately she'd noticed he'd taken to having a scotch or two before lunch—sometimes as early as 10:30. He glared at her now. She knew he was upset. She was messing up his tidy plans for the summer.

She probably shouldn't have told her parents anything at all. She probably should have listened to Tootie Ogilvie and had it taken care of as soon as she got home from school. Tootie, her oldest friend from first grade at Briarlee, had already had two abortions at the Women's Center downtown.

"They're good, Daph," Tootie had sworn. "You don't even feel it. Well, hardly. And they give you milk and cookies after it's all over. . . ."

Great, Daphne thought. Tootie made it sound like a birthday party. She might have gone along with Tootie's plan, except she kept changing her mind every minute.

To have it or not to have it? That was the question. The more she ruminated, the worse it got. Weeks slipped by.

Soon, she knew, it would be too late. Maybe that's what she wanted. . . .

"So what are you going to do?" Tootie had asked just yesterday. She couldn't understand

what all the fuss was about. But then, of course,
Tootie thought the baby was Freddie's.

Her parents were staring at her now, waiting
for her to say something. They, too, thought the
baby was Freddie's.

"I knew that boy was irresponsible," her father said, downing the last of his scotch. "I
warned you to stay away from him."

"For once your father is right, Daphne," said
her mother. "They're not our kind of people."

Who is? Daphne wondered. Both the Banks
and the Andrews families were monyeed. The
Andrews family, however, had made its fortune
prior to the Revolutionary War, while the
Bankses got rich in the gold rush of '49.

Daphne wondered with a chuckle what they
would think if they knew that the baby resting
in her womb was the grandchild of a Jewish
grocer from Flatbush Avenue in Brooklyn.

"This is no laughing matter, young lady!" her
father said impatiently, pouring himself another
scotch.

"Don't you think you've had enough to drink
already, Austin?" her mother asked him icily.

"I'll know when I've had enough!" her father
retorted.

"You *never* know when you've had enough,
Austin! You're very unpleasant when you're
drunk, do you know that?"

Daphne faded into the background as her parents went off on another of their famous shouting matches. In another minute they would forget she was even in the room.

She closed her eyes and thought of Bloom. If she and Bloom were married, they would never fight like this. What bliss it would be to be married to Bloom, to wake up each morning and touch him! Hear his voice . . .

But it would never be. Bloom was trapped in a loveless marriage to that cold fish of a wife of his, Nora Haddock Bloom.

She heard the telephone ring. In another moment Euvine came into the library and whispered to her, "It's Mr. Banks for you again, Miss Andrews. Shall I tell him you're out?"

Daphne stood up. "No, Euvine, I'll take it this time," she said, and tiptoed out of the room, leaving her parents still sniping at one another.

Freddie had been calling almost every day since she got home from Windsor. She'd been as honest as possible, under the circumstances.

"Freddie, I can't see you," she'd told him. "I've gotta think things through. . . ."

That wasn't good enough for him. "Think things through? What things?"

"Us," she said, improvising.

"Daphne—something's wrong. What is it?"

She'd become even more evasive, which had made Freddie all the more curious.

But it was true. She *did* have to sort things out. She knew Freddie was going to ask her to marry him sooner or later. It might as well be sooner.

But did she love him? She wasn't sure. One thing she did know, however: Life with him would never be dull, certainly not with his fast cars and his addiction to good times.

She picked up the phone in the foyer. "Hi, Freddykins," she said sweetly. "I miss you. When can I see you?"

"God, Daphne," he said, his voice cracking with emotion. "I'll be there in five minutes. . . ."

"Okay, girls," Iris Ledbetter was saying. "We have five minutes to catch the bus for the campus tour. Let's hustle."

Reluctantly, Daphne followed the others out into the bright sunshine. She had daydreamed away any chance of making it up to Bush Hill.

CHAPTER THIRTEEN

Bluma

Thank heaven they'd all finally left the dining room. Only eleven o'clock in the morning and she was totally exhausted. But then she'd hardly slept at all last night.

Uncle Ernesto's family was large and noisy. They'd kept her up late, wanting to talk, asking about her papa, her *abuelita*, about San Juan. . . .

Finally, they let her sleep. But the narrow cot they gave her in her cousin Conchita's room was hard as a rock. Worse, Conchita's baby, little Roberto, was teething and cried all night.

She'd had to be at the Elias Windsor Hall and Dining Facility by 6:30 A.M to help set up. At least Uncle Ernesto's house was close to the campus. It took only twenty minutes to walk to work.

She'd never seen such a big dining room! So

many tables! So many chairs! It was bigger even than the dining room in the hotel where her papa worked, except that there, in San Juan, the windows were so much cleaner!

Claudette, her boss, didn't like her from the start. "You de work-study girl?" The woman had scowled at her, foisting a starched white uniform onto her. "Dat's all I need! Anudder of dem uppity stupids!" Claudette muttered under her breath. To Bluma she said, "Put dis on quick! I ain't got no time for slowpokes!"

Bluma did as she was told. Back home nobody ever yelled at her. And certainly nobody ever called her stupid. And as far as she knew, she wasn't uppity in the least. How did this sour-faced woman ever get the idea that she was?

The uniform was at least four sizes too big for her, but Bluma didn't dare complain. At 6:45, as she hurried to set up the tables, curiosity got the better of her. "What's going on here today?" she asked Claudette.

"Some stupid reunion or sumpin'." Claudette shrugged. "Anytin' to give me extra work. . . ."

Another girl emerged from the kitchen and introduced herself. "Hi," she said to Bluma. "I'm Dwan. Welcome aboard." She set down a tray of silverware. When Claudette's back was turned Dwan stuck out her tongue and put her thumb to her nose.

Bluma giggled. "So this is a reunion, huh?"

Dwan looked puzzled. "Jeez, I don't know. I

think it's a dinner for some old professor who's leaving. . . ."

At that moment an extremely pale, thin woman, dressed all in black, entered the dining hall. Claudette suddenly was all smiles.

"Good mornin', Miz Bloom," she chirped. "So nice to see you heah dis early."

The woman didn't smile back. She crinkled her nose and peered into the kitchen. "Everything going according to schedule, Claudette? Has the coffee been made yet?"

Claudette threw Bluma a ferocious glance. "Get de coffee! From de cupboard! Fill de urn! *Quick!*"

Bluma scurried away. The woman in black gave her the creeps. There was something spooky about her. Abuelita would say the woman was *coco loco in the boco.*

Dwan poked her in the ribs. "That's *her,*" she said. "I mean, that's her husband that's retirin'. That's who the party's fer."

Without even knowing who the man was, Bluma felt sorry for him.

When the *coco loco* woman left, Claudette resumed her ill-tempered frenzy. "Toast! Toast! Don' let de toast burn!" she screamed.

Bluma, unnerved and trembling, left the coffee urns and flew to the toasters.

It was only later, after the dining hall had emptied out, that she realized she'd been using

the wrong-size coffee packets for the urns. *Mira!*
The coffee those poor women were drinking
was 90 percent water and 10 percent bean!
    She prayed they would not complain.

CHAPTER FOURTEEN

They were all here. All thirty-five of them.

His women.

She'd pulled it off!

She felt an odd sense of lightness, as though a great weight had been lifted from her shoulders. She supposed this was happiness. She began to hum as she hurried along the curving, elm-lined streets to the house.

"Who's sorry now?" she sang. "Da-da-da-dum-dum-de-da-da-da . . ."

She smiled and turned her key in the lock. This morning she'd risen at dawn, while he was still asleep. There were so many details to attend to! First, she had to make certain that breakfast would go as planned. She didn't want any of them asking too many questions. She'd been surprised when she saw that new girl helping Claudette in the kitchen. Hadn't she seen that girl last night, getting out of a limousine? She was almost sure of it. Well, who cared?

After tonight she'd never have to give a second thought to slutty girls like that. Wild, dark-haired women with enormous titties. Just his type! But then, what woman *wasn't* his type? Nora slammed the heavy front door shut behind her. She could feel the familiar claws grasping at her temples. She forced herself to stand straighter, to breathe deeply.

Why was she getting so upset? There was nothing to worry about any longer. After tonight she would be free.

The clock in the hall chimed eleven. They'd be getting on the bus now. She smiled. She'd thought of everything. *Everything.* Only eight more hours . . .

She climbed the stairs almost jauntily. The solid cherry wood of the bannister felt cool and reassuring beneath her hand. How she loved this house! How could Josiah believe for even a moment that she would ever leave it? That she would ever willingly live in Washington with him?

"You'll love it there, Nora," she mimicked his needling voice. "There are cherry blossoms and the Potomac and the Smithsonian. . . ."

Well, she *did* like the Smithsonian. But she didn't like it enough to desert this house. As she passed the portrait of her father, Philmont Haddock, the seventh president of Windsor College, she whispered, "Don't worry, Daddy dearest, I'll never leave this place. I'll never let strangers live in our house."

She entered the bedroom. Josiah was out jogging, as she knew he would be. Automatically she picked up his wet towel from the floor and tossed it into the hamper. She smiled, realizing she'd never have to clean up after Josiah Mendelsohn Bloom again.

In the bathroom the cap was off the toothpaste, as usual, and the water was dripping in the shower. To the world Josiah might be a revered genius, capable of walking on water. But she knew different. She knew the truth. Josiah Mendelsohn Bloom was nothing but a pig.

She peered through the lace curtain of her bedroom window. The yellow campus bus was just now lumbering down East Andrews Boulevard on its way to the tennis courts and the new swimming pool. How brilliant of her to have instructed the driver to take his time. There would be no chance of their seeing him as he navigated the campus on his idiotic run. They'd be there and he'd be here. He'd be there and they'd be here.

She smiled to herself. She had planned it all so well. She'd accomplished the impossible. She'd gathered his "flowers" together, brought them all here for the singular purpose of saying goodbye to him. She knew all about his precious wooden box and those ugly little cards. She had

long ago decoded their meaning. It was so easy
to slip their names onto that list of luminaries
invited to tonight's dinner. It was so easy to get
them rooms in the dorm. She giggled.

A little palm greasing, that's all it took. That,
and her status as wife of the great J. M. Bloom.
Those lackeys in the Office of Alumnae Affairs
would shine her shoes if she asked them to. She
giggled again.

They'd be saying good-bye, all right. *Good-
bye forever!*

She sat down on her side of the bed and
reached under her pillow for Teddy. Dear,
sweet Teddy.

Tears filled her eyes as she drew the stuffed
bear close. Her father had given Teddy to her on
her seventh birthday. "Teddy was *my* bear,"
he'd said lovingly, "and someday, Nora my darling, you'll give this bear to your own child."

Her own child . . .

"You're pregnant?"

Josiah looked stricken. The color had drained
from his face. In the late afternoon Amsterdam
sun the murky waters of the canal glistened with
an eely glow. "How can it be?"

She threw him a coy smile. "Come on, Josiah.
Don't tell me you don't know how babies are
made. . . ."

He frowned. "That's not what I mean and you

know it," he said impatiently. "I thought we—you—were being careful."

He was angrier than she'd ever seen him. For an instant she worried that she had gone too far. She laid her head on his chest. "Please don't be angry, Josiah," she cooed. She looked up at him. How she loved his hair! His beautiful, flaming hair. Red as the sunset. "You do love me, don't you?" she asked.

He didn't reply right away. Finally, his voice cracking, he said, "You know I do."

Without giving him a chance to say more, she told him, "We'll get married right away. And when you're finished with this silly tulip thing with Van Bergen, Daddy will get you a job at Windsor."

Why did he continue to hesitate? Why wasn't he taking her into his arms and covering her face with kisses, the way he'd done that first afternoon when they'd met in the café?

She never once doubted that he was the perfect man for her. He wasn't like the others. The others had merely used her for their own pleasure. And, she had to admit, she'd used them too. Used them and discarded them, just as they'd discarded her.

Josiah might be young, but he was more of a man than any man she'd ever known—except her daddy, of course. Josiah was kind. He was smart. But there was something more than that. Something elusive and tragic. She sensed that

Josiah had suffered some great sadness in his life.
In that way they had something in common.

And now Josiah had helped her prove that the
doctors were wrong. What did they know, anyway? The nerve of them telling her she could
never bear a child. Some idiotic nonsense about
being born without ovaries. *Pish tosh!* She'd
have a child if she damned well willed herself to
have one!

And so they were wed. And for three months
she'd known true happiness.

It was only when they'd returned to Tinguely
in September that things began to turn sour.

Her father was happy to have her home, married and settled at last. He accepted Josiah from
the start. "So. Nora tells me you're quite an extraordinary young man," he'd said to Josiah.
"Quite brilliant, it seems. Well, it so happens
that we've a place for a brilliant scholar in our
philosophy department."

Daddy had been *so* generous. Why hadn't
Josiah been more grateful? He had some absurd
notion of the two of them living off by themselves somewhere. But that was so silly. Why
live in a dinky little apartment when there was
so much room in Daddy's house?

It was their first real fight.

But, of course, Josiah capitulated. What choice
did he have?

* * *

Slowly their days settled into a kind of routine. Every morning before dawn Josiah would leave her bed. He had some crazy new hobby. He called it *running*. Aimless meandering was more like it.

"How can you run if you're not going anyplace?" she asked him.

"You don't understand," he said. "It's exhilarating. You should try it."

She clasped her hands protectively around her belly. "Don't be ridiculous," she said.

And so Josiah ran alone, to her eternal embarrassment. Everyone was whispering about him, she knew it. "The Runner," they called him behind his back. "The Runner's Wife," they called her. Again, she begged him to stop.

"Nora, darling, listen to me," he said. "This sort of exercise oxygenates the blood, *enriches* it, so to speak. It clears the mind of extraneous thought. In fact, I'm thinking of writing a book about it. . . ."

Even her own dear daddy fell victim to Josiah's obsession.

"I guarantee you'll love running, Philmont," Josiah had said, beaming, as Daddy laced up his new sneakers that fateful day.

"But, Daddy, are you sure?" she'd asked in concern. "You *never* do anything physical!"

But Josiah had cast his spell and Daddy was mesmerized.

It was a true New England autumn day. Late
October. The leaves on the trees were a fiery
orange and a blood-red. She watched the two
men in her life run side by side until they disappeared around the corner. Minutes later she
heard the shrill wail of an ambulance and knew
immediately what had happened.

"You've killed him! You've killed my daddy!"
she shrieked when a trembling Josiah came to
tell her the terrible news.

They called it a stroke. She called it murder.

She never totally forgave him. After the funeral, when she'd been at loose ends and had to
be hospitalized, Josiah visited her. She turned
away from him. If her hands had been free, she
would have scratched his eyes out.

"Please, Nora," Josiah had begged. "I had no
idea your father had a heart problem. I had no
idea. . . ."

She spat at him.

Eventually they'd made a kind of truce.

A hostile truce.

Now she rested her head against the pillow.
The house was so wonderfully quiet. How she
loved this time of the year when the campus
emptied out. Early summer. A time of hope.

For the first time in a long time, she felt at
peace.

She closed her eyes. She could feel herself

drifting away. But no. She didn't want to sleep quite yet. Tonight, after it was all over, she would sleep. Deeply. Peacefully. The way *he* slept. Never again would she be disrupted by his terrible snoring or, worse, the talking. Yes, the "genius" talked in his sleep! And he said only one word over and over again. . . .

The first time she'd heard the name Estrella she'd been merely curious. By the sixth or seventh time, however, she couldn't help but ask, "Who's Estrella?"

They were in the middle of breakfast. His hand trembled. Calmly, she wiped up the spilled coffee and pinned him with her eyes.

And waited.

When he could speak he stammered, "Wh-wh-where did you hear that name?"

She raised an eyebrow. "From you," she replied coolly. "You talk in your sleep, you know."

He started to say something, then thought better of it.

She forced herself to sound nonchalant. "Well," she said, "don't tell me if you don't think it's important." She held her breath.

When he did reply his voice was strained. "Estrella," he whispered. "Estrella." It was an embrace. "She was someone I knew once, long ago. But I lost her." His voice trailed.

"Did you love her?"

"Very much," he said huskily.

She gasped.

"I'm not trying to be cruel, Nora," he said kindly, "but you asked. I met her when I was very young. Before I met you. . . ."

How young could he have been? Nora wondered. He was only nineteen when they married!

"Was she beautiful?" Nora persisted. "Was she as beautiful as I am?"

He nodded. "When I first saw you in the café in Amsterdam, I thought you were she," he admitted softly.

Nora clamped her hands over her ears. "No more!" she screamed. "I don't want to hear another word about your damned Estrella!"

And she hadn't. Except at night, three or four times a week when he talked in his sleep.

But after tonight she would never hear the name Estrella again.

She sat up in bed. From downstairs she could hear the grandfather clock begin to chime. *Noon.* In exactly ten minutes he would be back. All sweaty and dirty from his "fun." His fun run. She would stop his fun run with the gun.

Slowly her hand reached around Teddy's back and found the zipper. Her fingers probed Teddy's soft insides and settled on the cool metal.

She pulled it out. It was so pretty. So delicate. Her little pearl-handled revolver. It fit so neatly in the palm of her hand.

She'd happened on it quite by accident, almost a year after Daddy's death. It was right there, in the middle drawer of Daddy's desk, already loaded.

She'd kept it all these years, knowing that the time would eventually come when she would need it.

The time was now.

CHAPTER FIFTEEN

Bloom

He couldn't catch his breath. What was happening? He'd run halfway up Bush Hill and had had to turn around. Gasping for air, he'd stumbled and nearly fallen.

He wished with all his heart he could have seen the cave just one last time before leaving campus. The cave held so many memories for him. How fortuitous to have happened upon it. How appropriate that he, a philosopher, like Plato, should have a special place to ponder, to meditate, to unravel the mysteries of life. A place in which to love. . . .

Some of the sweetest moments of his life had been lived in that cave. His Nora-free moments.

He ambled slowly back toward the house. His left arm felt heavy and strange, as if some demon were pricking it with pins and needles. It must be from all the exertion of the last few days, all the packing, the lifting of the cartons, the handling of so many heavy books.

He lifted his right arm and wiped his forehead. He was sweating like a *glos tay,* as his mother would say. A glass of tea.

His mother. He would be seeing her in a few hours. His sister Rochelle too. He felt a stab of sorrow that they hadn't been close for so many years. But then, it had taken all his powers to forgive them. To this day they had never admitted it, but he knew they were responsible for coming between him and the love of his life, Estrella DeSouza.

He'd dreamed about her again last night. His Estrella. She was so real this time, he could almost reach out and touch her! In fact, in the dream he *did* touch her; he actually felt the soft cotton of her luminous panties. When he'd awakened he realized that he'd had a wet dream. He'd turned guiltily to see if Nora had noticed, but she wasn't even there. At that moment he'd felt a mixture of relief and surprise. The clock on the table told him it was 5:30— early, even for his crazy insomniac of a wife, who never slept more than two hours a night, tops.

Where could she be off to at this hour? But he'd learned not to ask too many questions about Nora's behavior. He knew she would be back. She never liked to leave the house for long. That's why he was surprised when she had so compliantly agreed to move to Washington.

Maybe, at long last, she *was* getting better.

He rounded the corner of Andrews Boulevard. His breath was still forced. He felt the same dull ache in his chest. He willed himself to think about tonight, about all the friends and colleagues he would see.

Had Nora remembered to pick up his tux from the cleaners? He'd left her several little notes—on the refrigerator, on the bathroom mirror, on the grandfather clock in the hall. He wanted to look his best tonight. He wanted his last official appearance on the Windsor College campus to be memorable.

He felt a sharp jab of pain between his ribs. *Don't give in to it,* he told himself. He concentrated instead on the guest list, the one he'd painstakingly put together and handed to Nora to expedite. Jonas would be coming. Carl, too. Henry and Nancy. Isaac, of course. And Max Miller. He'd heard that Max had remarried. A beautiful *shiksa* this time. He hoped that Max would be luckier with *his* shiksa than he'd been with Nora. . . .

Max's wife had gone to Oslo with him when he'd won his Nobel last year, even though she was pregnant out to here. Lucky Max, to have a wife who could bear him children. What had he, Josiah Mendelsohn Bloom, ever done to be denied the fundamental joy of fatherhood?

But of course Nora had never told him the truth. He'd believed her when she'd said she was pregnant. He'd married her believing that. He had actually seen her belly grow—or thought he had. How shocked, how horrified he'd been, then, when he'd learned the truth—that Nora had *never* been pregnant, could *never* be pregnant, would *never* bear a child.

After her father's death, when Nora had fallen to pieces, it was the doctor who told him.

"A false pregnancy," the doctor had explained. "Very common among hysterics. . . ."

Josiah had been rendered speechless. He looked up to find the doctor watching him closely. "Dr. Bloom? Are you all right?"

He wasn't all right. The waiting-room walls were spinning. This doctor wasn't making any sense! Nora—an hysteric? Wasn't that the traditional term for the seriously disturbed?

The doctor was still talking. "It's unfortunate her father had to die at this time. You know her history of course . . . ?"

Josiah shook his head. He didn't know her history. He'd assumed Nora was as normal as anyone. That at times she seemed slightly off center he'd attributed to the fact that she was—well—a WASP. She was a dyed-in-the-wool Protestant from New England; he was a lowly *litvak* from Flatbush Avenue. There were cultural differences. How was he to know she was crazy?

Josiah looked at the doctor. "You mean she's not going to have my baby?"

The doctor shook his head. "She's not going to have anyone's baby. It's called Turner Syndrome." He paused. He gestured wordlessly for a moment. "She has no . . . no, uh . . ."

"Female equipment?" Josiah finished.

"You got it." The doctor lowered his eyes.

"I don't believe it," Josiah whispered.

"I was sure you knew Mrs. Bloom's history," the doctor said. "You met her in Amsterdam, right? Surely you knew that ZuDreitn Haus was for recovering schizophrenics?"

It was all too much.

But the doctor wasn't finished.

"I must make it clear that Nora will need your continued support now more than ever. Even though, at times, she will seem to be perfectly lucid . . ."

He only half-listened. He would divorce her. Find a woman who could give him the child he so desperately wanted. But no. The doctor was saying, "Any drastic action on your part could send her reeling over the edge for good."

So there it was. His conundrum. He sighed, ruing the day he'd seen her, sitting there in the café in Amsterdam, with her long beautiful legs and that wild black hair blowing in the wind. So like his beloved Estrella . . .

He shuffled up the flagstone path to the house. From the corner of his eye he saw a yellow campus bus turn toward the Humanities Quadrangle. Strange. It was too early for the summerschool students to be on campus. Too late for this year's students.

But it didn't matter. After tonight Josiah Mendelsohn Bloom would be on his way to immortality.

CHAPTER SIXTEEN

Revelations

Vinnie had been under the car for hours now. He was going nowhere fast.

Well, it sure wasn't the carburetor. Maybe the cam shaft? Maybe the fuel line? Maybe, maybe, maybe . . . maybe he should quit and admit he'd failed again. What did a roofer know about cars anyway?

His left big toe was itching like a son-of-a-gun. The famous toe that wasn't there. "Phantom sensations," the doctor called them. "Just memories. Your brain is remembering how the toe used to itch."

"Doesn't my brain know there's no more foot?"

The doctor had refused to answer that one. Damn the doctors anyway. What do they know? All they knew was how to drive you crazy with bills!

The screen door slammed. From where he lay beneath the car Vinnie could see Jace's ratty old sneakers coming toward him. God, how he wished he could buy the kid a pair of those fancy running shoes for $35 like his brother-in-law Sean bought for his kids.

"Dad? Is that you under there?"

Who else would be under this heap? Vinnie thought. Who else would have only one foot sticking out?

Aloud he said, "Yup! Hey, Jace, wanna hand me that wrench?"

Jace was staring at him in admiration. "Gee, Dad, how'd you ever find that fuel leak? It's amazing!"

Vinnie took another gulp from the diet soda and wiped his mouth with the back of his hand. Amazing was right, he thought. Amazing *luck!* Jace didn't know it, of course, but he'd been about to give up on the car when suddenly he felt something wet drip on his forehead. Sure enough, there was a pinprick in the fuel line. All he had to do was plug it up. He took the gum out of his mouth and that was it! Bingo!

He'd started the car and, sure enough, the damn thing was purring like a pussycat. Jace whooped. They'd hugged each other as if Vinnie had just hit a grand slam with two men out in the bottom of the ninth.

It was the first time he'd been alone with Jace

in a long time. Without Chrystal or the girls to run interference. They sat at the kitchen table without having to say anything to each other. No forced conversation. Just smiles.

Jace really was a good kid, even though he was smart. To look at him you'd never guess he was nearly through with high school at the age of thirteen. He didn't look like one of those whiz kids. Except for the glasses of course.

"Hey, listen, Dad. My history teacher, Mr. Shrubsole, has been having a lot of trouble with his car. Maybe you could help him out. . . ."

Vinnie started to say, "Who, me?" but then he thought about it. Why *not* him? He'd fixed the old Chevy, hadn't he? Maybe he had a natural talent that he'd never even known about. "Sure. Why not?" he said. "I'll have a look-see. Tell him to bring the car over anytime."

Jace beamed. "Gee, Dad, that's great. You really mean it?"

Sure he really meant it. He had promised himself that he was going to turn over a new leaf, and so far so good. He hadn't had a beer in how many hours? Twenty-four! He hadn't even turned on the television set! And he had a shirt on, and he had fixed the car.

And now he was going to look at Jace's teacher's car. Who knew where it could lead? To Jace he said, "Go on, kid. Call your teacher."

He watched Jace jump up and run to the phone. Too bad the kid didn't look more like a

Malatesta. But then, how could he? He *wasn't* a
Malatesta! Whatever lowlife had knocked
Chrystal up all those years ago must have been
some *face brute!* The guy must have been Irish
with red hair like that. An Irishman with a
schnozz big enough to blow bubbles with.

Still, the guy must have had *something* going
for him to get Chrystal into the sack. God knows,
he, himself, had tried for years to get into her
pants with no success. She'd been a virgin when
she'd left Boonton Harbor for that hoity-toity
school, he would swear it.

His Chrystal. How he loved her. He looked at
the yellow clock on the wall. Noon. She'd been
gone since yesterday morning and how he
ached to have her back with him. What was she
doing this very minute? His wife. His *bella
ragazza.*

Jace appeared, looking disappointed. "No answer at Mr. Shrubsole's," he said.

Vinnie smiled at the boy. So what if he wasn't
really his? He loved him like his own. "I got a
good idea," Vinnie said. "Now that the car's running, why don't we go out and get us a pizza?"

The look of happiness on Jace's face was answer enough.

Biffy sounded pissed.

"What do you mean you're not coming over?
I've already made the pinã coladas! I've already

made the salad! The tofu patties are already on the grill!"

Tofu patties? Vey iss mir! "Biffy, baby, try to understand! I wouldn't be good company tonight. My back is still out." Kermit had swallowed enough painkillers to put a horse to sleep, but his sacroiliac was still on fire. If he moved even a finger, he felt it in his spine. The last thing he needed now was a *shtupp* with Biffy Barclay.

"K.O., I know what your problem is. You don't get enough exercise. Just listen. Get down on the floor . . . Kermie? Are you on the floor?"

"Yes, doll," he groaned. He *was* on the floor. In fact, he hadn't been able to get *off* the floor in a day and a night. He held the receiver away from his ear and closed his eyes. He could hear Biffy coaching: "Fifty push-ups, K.O. Starting . . . *now!* Up, down, up, down, up, down . . . K.O.? Feeling any better?"

"Better," he said dully. Who did she think she was—Jane Fonda? Enough monkey business. "This isn't going to work, doll," he said finally. "I'll call you in the morning. . . ."

"But—"

He hung up. He hated to admit it, but the novelty of *shtupping* Biffy Barclay had worn thin. At one time those incredible knockers and that juicy twat would have been enough to keep him happy. But lying on the floor here in agony for a night and a day had given him time to think. There was more to life than tit and twat. Like love, for instance. And loyalty, for instance. And a couple of other important "for instances" that Biffy Barclay would never understand.

God, he missed his Rosalie. Why hadn't she called? He closed his eyes and saw her: the sparkling, intelligent eyes; the warm, caring smile. The sharp wit. His Rosalie wouldn't make him do push-ups in his condition.

She was some smart cookie, his Rosalie. She would know in a minute that *Yesterday's News* wasn't worth a dime and that he should get out now, before another fourteen mil got flushed down the tubes. . . .

He heard the downstairs door slam. He froze in panic. He wished now that he hadn't given Sedilla the weekend off. Suppose it was another Charlie Manson, some maniac on the loose, come to trash him? And here he was, helpless, like a baby, unable to move.

The thing was coming up the stairs. "Who's there?" he called hoarsely. No answer. "Rosalie?" he ventured. Still no answer.

The bedroom door opened.

"It's only me, Daddy . . ." Josie's voice trailed off. "What are you doing on the floor?"

She walked over to him and knelt down.

Kermit tried to smile. "It's just my back, honey," he managed to say. He remembered that she'd slept overnight at her friend Melo-

die's house. "How's Melodie?" he asked duti-
fully.

Josie didn't answer immediately. When she
finally did answer her voice sounded strained.
"Okay, I guess."

She guessed? Something wasn't right. She
looked funny. Like she'd been crying. "What's
wrong, honey?" he asked.

"Nothing," she said. A moment passed. *"Everything,"* she said, bursting into tears.

Uh-oh! In his lexicon "everything" could
mean only one thing: The boys were giving her
a hard time. Not that he could exactly blame
them. That $10,000 nose job of hers had
changed Josie from a plain Jane into a fancy
Frances.

He held out his hand and she took it. "Tell
Daddy," he urged gently. "Tell me, *bub-
bele. . . ."*

She sniffled and grabbed a tissue from the mirrored tissue holder on the floor next to him. She
studied her reflection for a long minute and
shook her head. "It's not what I thought it would
be," she said miserably.

Kermit forced himself to remain calm. Some
creep had obviously gotten into her pants. He'd
kill the bastard! "Yeah," he commiserated, "it
never is." What should he say now? Should he
try to find out the guy's name? Would she tell
him?

Rosalie never told him. Not once in seventeen

years had she divulged the identity of Josie's real father. Instead, whenever they even got near the subject, she clammed up like the petals of those damn roses she got every year on her birthday.

He thought about those roses. Mystery roses from her mystery man. It was like living with Brenda Starr and a phantom Basil St. John!

Josie cried, "I wanna go back to the way it was. . . ."

He shook his head. Was it like this for every girl the first time? "I'm sorry, honey," he said softly, his heart aching for her. "It just can't be done. I mean, once it's gone, it's gone. . . ."

She turned toward him, her newly beautiful face awash in sadness. "Melodie told me her cousin found a doctor who could do it. Put it back, I mean."

Kermit's eyes widened in surprise. What next? he wondered. Was there no limit to the wonders of modern science? "But . . . Josie," he bumbled. "What's the point? I mean, face it. It's not the stigma it used to be. . . ."

She gave him a dark look. "I knew you wouldn't understand."

He understood all too well. Someone had taken advantage of his innocent little girl. "Tell me his name," he demanded.

She brightened. "Just a minute, Daddy. I wrote it down. . . ."

His jaw dropped. *She had to write it down?*

She didn't even know the boy well enough to remember his name?

Josie dug into the pocket of her jeans and came up with a folded scrap of paper. "Dr. Morton J. Feldman," she chirped.

Kermit's heart began to pound. It was worse than he thought! *A doctor!* He would have the bastard's license revoked! "I'll kill the sonofabitch!" he screamed, forgetting why he was lying on the floor in the first place. The sharp pain in his lower back reminded him with a vengeance.

Josie paled and backed away. "Kill him?" she repeated incredulously. "Why would you want to kill him? I *need* him!"

The pain was hitting him from all angles now. He grimaced. "Need him?" he managed to say. "The bastard seduces you and you *need* him?"

Josie, hands on hips, stared at him. *"Seduces?* What are you talking about? I don't even know Dr. Feldman!"

Kermit couldn't believe what he was hearing. "My God, Josie. You do it with someone you don't even know?"

"Do it? Do *what?* Dr. Feldman can give me my old nose back. Melodie's cousin had a really bad nose job and Dr. Feldman fixed it so she looked just like she used to. And she's very, *very* happy! I know I would be, too, because, Daddy, I don't know who I am anymore!"

It was too much for him to take in all at once.

So it wasn't a boy, after all. It was a nose. The nose attracted the boys, but the boys didn't get in.

"Just because I have a new nose doesn't mean that I'm a new person, does it? I'm the same old Josie, no matter what I look like. But the boys don't understand! They all want me to do— *things*. You know . . ." She blushed and looked away.

The relief he felt was palpable. Tears came into his eyes. The poor kid. No one had prepared her for the bum's rush that had come with the new nose.

It was his fault. After all, he'd been the one to go along with Josie's pleas to have her nose done. It was Rosalie who had held back. How wise she was, his Rosalie.

"I love you, Josie, no matter what your nose looks like." He reached out and pulled her close and gave her a warm, paternal hug. "Don't you worry, sweetie pie. It's gonna be all right. Everything's gonna be all right. . . ."

She gave him a trembly little smile. "I wish Mom were here," she said.

Kermit sighed. "So do I, Josie love. So do I."

Erich Reinisch puffed majestically on his intricately carved meerschaum pipe. "Zo. Zid? Yah?"

Sid couldn't think of anything else to say. He'd already said it all.

Just thinking about the dream made him sweat all over again. Daphne driving off into the sunset in his Land Rover never to be seen again.

He bit into the cuticle on his thumb and winced. If he didn't settle this thing about Daphne, he wasn't going to have any cuticles left at all. He was a nervous wreck. He'd been waiting a full thirty hours for her to call. And she hadn't. "I can't get her out of my mind," he said.

"Zo-o-o," Reinisch prodded. "Vat do you put togedder from ziss?"

Sid didn't want to think about it. The whole thing was too much for him to contemplate. "What can I say?" he said. "I've gotten involved with a patient. I've violated a basic tenet of our profession."

Reinisch made a face. "Nah, nah, bezides dot," he said, with a wave of his hand.

Sid looked up in shock. "What do you mean *besides* that?"

Reinisch stroked his beard and considered. "Ziss iss a departure for you, yah?"

"Yes! I've never so much as laid a hand on a patient before! I'll never do it again! But this time—I—I . . ." He was sweating bullets. He pulled a handkerchief from his pocket and wiped his brow. He cleared his throat. "But Daphne—she seemed so alone, so confused, so . . ."

"Zo. Ziss iss no mere zexual ezcapade . . . ?"

Sidney shook his head wildly. "Of course not!
I—"

"Yah?" Reinisch encouraged, leaning forward.
"Get it out, mein boy. . . ."

Sidney stood up. His mouth opened. Why was
it so hard for him to say a simple, four-letter
word? Men said it all the time. Mothers said it to
babies. Babies said it to mothers. Old people said
it to young people. Young people said it to each
other. The Bible was full of it. *What was the
matter with him?*

Reinisch was scribbling madly on that infernal
pad of his.

Sidney closed his eyes and pictured her: that
beautiful face, those big blue eyes, those innocent lips, those long legs that went up to her—
"Love! I *love* her, Doctor! I, Sidney Funt, M.D.,
am head over heels in love with Daphne Banks!"

Reinisch was giving him a radiant smile.
"Louder, Zid!"

"I LOVE HER! I LOVE DAPHNE ANDREWS
BANKS AND I WANT TO MARRY HER!"

Reinisch was standing too. "Bravo!" he ap-
plauded. "Ziss is real progress, no?"

CHAPTER SEVENTEEN

Lunch

Time had not touched the Tinguely Inn.

It was still just as dingy and run-down as ever. Townies still hogged the barstools up front, nursing their boilermakers and keeping a dull eye on the never-ending ball game.

The back room still belonged, by and large, to the girls of Windsor. Windowless and smelling of stale beer and staler perfume, it was meant to hold no more than twenty-five people, tops. All thirty-five of them were sitting elbow to elbow now, at small, scarred tables. The jukebox, as usual, was out of order.

In the far corner, next to the men's room, where the old pinball machine used to be, a video game now stood. Three grungy, tattooed boys hovered around the bleeping green screen, seemingly oblivious to the Windsor contingent.

Rosalie squirmed uncomfortably on the rickety wooden chair. They were packed in like sardines. Wall-to-wall women. Something was bothering her. She had counted thirty-five, including that pretty blonde named Daisy, who'd arrived after breakfast this morning.

Why weren't more of Bloom's students here? After all, he'd been teaching for more than thirty years.

And something else. She had the eerie feeling that this entire weekend was being orchestrated by an unseen hand.

A buzzing fly zoomed in and settled on the rim of her water glass. She flicked it away. But the fly came back and dived right into the water.

"Gross," said Daphne, who was sitting next to her. "Ask the waitress to get you another glass."

Chrystal smiled wryly. "First we have to get the waitress. Which, if memory serves, is easier said than done in this place."

Rosalie laughed lightly. She found herself enjoying the company of Daphne and Chrystal. It was an unexpected bonus. There was something about them. They were Windsor girls, of course, but it was more than that. Rosalie sensed that they had something else in common, but she didn't know what.

The waitress finally came to take their orders.

"Well, it's about time," Iris Ledbetter growled. "Give me a brandy and a quiche and brewed decaffeinated," she commanded.

The waitress, a scrawny redhead with acne

scars, cracked her gum. "A beer an' a quiche? We ain't got quiche. We ain't got brewed decaffeinated, either. Ya's got yer cherce of weiners on a bun or chipped beef on toast."

Iris stared. "I don't believe this," she said. "I came twenty-five hundred miles for shit on a shingle?"

The waitress tapped her foot. "Take it or leave it, lady."

Iris opted for the weiner.

When it came Daphne's turn she quietly asked, "Would it be possible to get a Scrumptious Yogurt?"

The waitress, pad in hand, started to say, "I already tol' ya's . . ." Then she took a closer look at Daphne. "Oh, jeez! You're *her*!" She jumped up and down excitedly and thrust the order pad under Daphne's nose. "Hey, could I get your autograph? For my kid?"

Obligingly, Daphne scrawled her name.

The boys around the video machine turned around. "Who's she?" one of them asked loud enough for the women to hear.

"Who knows?" said another.

"She ain't Madonna, that's fer sure," said the third boy, turning his attention back to the video game.

After the waitress left, Iris turned to Daphne. "My God. How can you stand it? You can't even go into a goddamn bar without being molested by an autograph hound! That's why I've never wanted to be in the public eye."

"And I'm sure you've had many opportunities . . ." Rosalie said to Iris.

Daphne wanted to disappear. She shouldn't have come here for lunch. Why hadn't she followed her instincts and tried to find Bloom? She suspected that tonight he would be so deluged by well-wishers, she wouldn't get a chance to say two words to him. It was almost as though someone was deliberately trying to keep her away from him. . . .

The din in the back room rose steadily.

Chrystal had another headache. She wished Iris would shut up.

"I just love reunions," Iris said loudly, guzzling her beer.

Chrystal reminded her, "This isn't really a reunion, Iris. I mean, the reason we're all here is to say good-bye to Professor Bloom." At the mention of his name the women fell oddly silent. A wistful smile softened Iris's sharp features.

"I always think of him as just plain Bloom," said Iris.

Someone at another table dropped a spoon. A few of them cleared their throats. Women all over the room began to fidget.

"Funny, but I do too," said Rosalie.

Chrystal looked at her. "Me, too," she said.

"And me," said Daphne.

Someone changed the subject. "Let me show

you pictures of my kids," said Violetta Trubenik, at the next table.

Iris immediately fished in her purse and came up with a handful of photographs. "This is my Jeremy," she announced proudly. "Only thirty-four years old and already head of the Geology Department at Harvard." She passed the picture around.

Rosalie waited while Daphne, and then Chrystal, examined the photos. They seemed to be giving them a lot of attention, scrutinizing them for long moments until, finally, they passed them on to her.

She riffled through them. Jeremy was clearly not a handsome man, not in the classical sense, anyway. He was rather homely, in fact, with red, kinky hair and piercing blue eyes staring from behind horn-rimmed glasses. He had a large—a *very* large—nose. A nose like Josie used to have. . . .

Iris, obviously pleased at the attention her son's photo was generating, volunteered more information: "He's one of the top rock men in the entire world." She paused, waiting for it to sink in.

Rosalie was riveted on Jeremy's nose. There was something about that face, the expression in the eyes—where had she seen it before?

"Let me see that again," Chrystal said, pulling the photos from Rosalie's hand.

"Me, too," said Daphne.

"Well, come on, girls," Iris said, pleased. "Let's see pictures of *your* kids. . . ."

And so it had begun.

"These are my four," said Chrystal absently. "The twins, Heather and Maria. Theresa, my older girl . . ."

But Daphne's eyes were fixed on the boy.

"That's Jace," said Chrystal.

Jace was red-haired. He wore glasses. His eyes were piercingly blue. His nose was large. *Very* large.

"Let me see," said Rosalie. She stared at the picture of Jace for a long time. Then she passed it to Iris, who stared at it too.

Soon, all over the room, women were scrutinizing photographs of each other's children.

Finally, Daphne produced her own pictures. "This is my Josh," Daphne said weakly. Her fingertips were numb. Her stomach was doing flipflops. Something was going on here—something she didn't want to think about.

She picked up the picture of Rosalie's daughter and sighed with relief. Yes, Rosalie's Josie had red hair. Yes, she had blue eyes. But she was beautiful.

Chrystal, too, took another look at Josie's picture. "She's really beautiful, Rosalie," she said, smiling.

Then Iris had another look. She stared intently at Josie's picture, as if looking for something that wasn't there. "Very pretty girl," she conceded finally. And then she looked up at Rosalie.

"And a damn good nose job."

CHAPTER EIGHTEEN

After Lunch

Chrystal couldn't remember leaving the Tinguely Inn. She dimly recalled going back to her room in the dorm, taking off her good shoes, putting on her old sneakers.

Here she was, now, halfway up Bush Hill, trying to make sense of it.

She shook her head. *No. It couldn't be.* It was a trick of the lighting in that stupid back room, that's what it was. That and too much beer. Besides, after a while, don't all kids begin to look alike?

No, they don't, said a nagging voice within her.

Her eyes were burning from lack of sleep. Her stomach grumbled. "Lots of kids have red hair," she said aloud, breaking the heavy silence of the hills.

She could feel the sharp edges of the pebbles

pushing through the worn soles of her sneakers.
How odd to be up here again after all this time!
The winding trail that led to the cave looked the
same. Only she was different now. So much had
happened to change her. . . .

Bloom's words reverberated in her mind.
"Your breasts are magnificent, my sweet chrysanthemum," he had crooned as his lips closed
gently around her nipple. "My own, my only
chrysanthemum . . ."

Chrystal shook her head. *It can't be true!* she
thought. *It can't possibly be true!*

She ran the rest of the way. Where else to go
but to their own private haven, their sanctuary?
She'd felt the pull of this place since she'd arrived, and she could no longer resist.

What was that poem he'd recited to her that
last time? "All night upon mine heart, I felt her
warm heart beat . . ." She knew it was Dow-
son, but which poem? No matter. He'd loved
her. She was sure of it.

Those pictures of the kids . . . It was mere
coincidence that they looked so much alike.

Daphne squinted in the bright afternoon sunlight. Where had she left her sunglasses? God
only knew. It was a miracle she was able to func-
tion at all.

As soon as she'd left that horrible luncheon
and vomited, she'd washed her face and taken a

deep drink of water. Still, she could actually taste the implications of what had transpired.

She was almost there. Brambles scratched at her ankles as she made her way up Bush Hill. She clenched her fists. All those photographs. All those carbon-copy kids. What did it mean?

Maybe nothing. Sid would probably say she was overreacting.

But was she? Bloom had loved her. "My sweet, bright daffodil," he'd said so often. "You bring sunshine into the darkest crevices of my being. You. Only you have given me such happiness. . . ."

Only her?

All these years she'd never once doubted that he'd loved only her.

But how about all those pictures?

Well, maybe the answer would come once she reached the cool, dark serenity of the cave.

That Iris Ledbetter sure had a big mouth, thought Rosalie as she climbed the pebbly path. She should have changed her shoes, but who could think at a time like this? Maybe she was dreaming. Maybe she would wake up and find that today hadn't happened.

But she knew better.

The heel of her shoe caught in some pebbles. She held on to a vine to keep from falling. She looked down. The campus looked peaceful, idyllic. Well, so much for appearances . . .

Oh God, what was she going to do? Suppose it was true? Suppose those pictures told the truth? Suppose Bloom hadn't loved only her?

"My singular, fragile rose, how I love you, how I adore you, only you. You alone give me the sustenance to continue on this barren earth. . . ."

How she had clung to the memory of those words. But suppose it was all an illusion?

Wearily, she continued to climb. Surely, there was a logical explanation. It had been dark in the Tinguely Inn. She was exhausted. Her brain was starved for oxygen. She could have been hallucinating. . . .

Couldn't she?

CHAPTER NINETEEN

Armageddon

Chrystal eased herself in between the boulders. Immediately she was enveloped in the cool, dark solitude of the cave. She placed the flat of her hand against the wall. Its solidity reassured her.

She sighed and closed her eyes. She had to think.

What would Bloom make of all this? First, she knew, he would consider the facts. Then he would try to put them in some sort of logical order. Then he would attempt to draw a hypothesis.

According to the old truth tables Bloom had often referred to, if you start out with a true statement and then make a false assumption, the conclusion would always be false. If, on the other hand, the statement is true and the assumption is equally true, the conclusion has to be true. Was she doing this right?

She thought she heard a sound from somewhere in the depths of the cave. She listened harder. Nothing.

Fact, Chrystal thought: We all have children with red hair and prominent noses—all except Rosalie, that is, and her Josie had a nose job.

She paused, unwilling to make the obvious assumption. She began to pace slowly back and forth from one side of the cave to the other. The acrid smell of moist earth assailed her senses. How well she remembered that smell. "Nectar of the gods," Bloom had said, inhaling deeply. "The attar of heaven."

Statement: Bloom has red hair and a prominent nose. Statement: He teaches at Windsor. Statement: We were all his students. . . . She couldn't go on.

From out of the darkness a voice suddenly boomed, "What the hell are you doing here?"

Chrystal's heart lurched. Peering into the black space before her, she said, "Iris? Is that *you*?"

Iris emerged slowly. She was sniffling. "Fuck. I didn't want to believe it, but—"

But before she could finish her sentence, two more forms squeezed themselves in between the boulders.

Rosalie's eyes darted from Iris to Chrystal to Violetta Trubenik, who had caught up with her just as she'd reached the cave. "What's going on here?" Rosalie asked. But she already knew.

Violetta, a short, roundish brunette with full lips and a heaving bosom, sputtered, "I don't know what you gals are doing here, but please be advised, this is a *private* cave!"

"Private, my ass!" Iris blurted huffily. "He brought me here when you were still in diapers!"

"Liar!" Violetta screamed. "He *never* brought you here!"

"He did too!" Iris screamed back, lunging toward Violetta.

"Did not!"

At that Iris and Violetta grabbed each other's hair and fell with a thud to the mossy floor of the cave.

"Ladies! Please! Stop!" Rosalie begged, trying in vain to separate the two women.

Behind them three more figures eased between the boulders.

Daphne looked around, her eyes growing accustomed to the dim light of the cave. Iris was sitting on the floor, pressing a tissue to her bleeding forehead. Next to her sat Violetta Trubenik, who was holding a large wad of Iris's steely gray hair in her hand.

"Shitsky," Daphne cursed softly. She turned to Rosalie. "What on earth's going on here?"

Rosalie didn't answer.

Within fifteen minutes it had gotten pretty crowded in the cave. They were all there. All thirty-five of them.

"This isn't happening," said Posy O'Toole, Class of '67.

"You wish," said Daphne. She pinched herself, hard. No luck. Here she was, after all these years, back in their secret place. But here were all the others too. She visualized Bloom with all these other women and broke into tears. She was aware that other women were sobbing as well. Had it all been a lie? An illusion? What about the daffodil he sent her every year on her birthday? What about the poem? She got up and groped along the walls, in the darkness, trying to find it.

Chrystal, watching her, asked, "Daphne, what *are* you doing?"

"I'm looking for something," Daphne said, distractedly.

"Looking for what? A contact lens?" Iris asked, bitchily.

And then she found it. The very words Bloom had chiseled for her and her alone. "I found it!" she declared in triumph. "He wrote this for me! It's proof that he loved me!" Huskily, she began to recite the lovely words that Bloom had etched on the wall after their final lovemaking:

"Golden are the strands of the daffodil's love,
  They windeth midst the branches of mine
      own
  Pure heart . . ."

"Oh, no! That's not right," Rosalie interrupted, groping along the opposite wall. "This is how it goes," she cried:

> "Red are the petals of the lovely rose,
>   They falleth midst the branches of
>   Mine own pure heart . . ."

Chrystal crawled over the sitting bodies of the others. "Now just you wait a minute, Rosalie Fineberg! It goes like this," she said, finding *her* poem on the wall of the cave.

> "The chrysanthemum's amber glow
>   Feeds these hungry branches of
>   Mine own pure . . ."

Iris stood up and screamed, *"Enough already! I got the same lousy poem. It's over there somewhere," she said, gesturing to the rear of the cave. "I was reading it when you so rudely interrupted me," she said to Chrystal.

Chrystal's knees had turned to rubber. Her heartbeat echoed emptily in her ears. So much for truth tables, she thought. Resignedly, she sighed and turned to the others. "What do we do now?" she asked.

Minutes went by and no one answered. Above their heads the patch of sky grew as dark as their thoughts.

Lilah Hassad, Class of '78, picked up a pebble

from the cave floor and flung it carelessly against the wall.

Gladys Kupferberg, Class of '73, stood up and did the same.

Within seconds thirty-three other women picked up pebbles and flung them against the walls of the cave.

And then, the pebbles insufficient for her fury, Iris Ledbetter picked up a large rock, balanced it in her hands, and then flung it against a wall with all her might. It shattered into tiny fragments that rained like tears onto the floor of the cave.

"Let's get out of this evil place!" she ordered.

And so, one by one, the women squeezed through the boulders into the twilight of Bush Hill. Shivering, sobbing, they gathered into a tight knot of misery in the cool evening air.

"Let's close it up!" commanded Iris. "Let's seal his damned cave! Seal it forever!"

Trembling from the horrendous revelations of the afternoon, Rosalie stared at Iris. "Are you *crazy*? We could *never* move those boulders! They must weigh a ton!"

For the first time in hours, Iris smiled. "Never say never, Rosalie. I know a little about rocks from my Jeremy. You have to know where to push. If you know that, a mouse could move a mountain. . . ."

Without another word, the women began to

push. Push and heave. Heave and shove. Again and again and again.

Slowly, *very* slowly, the boulder began to move. The entrance to the cave grew smaller and smaller and smaller, until, finally, it was no more.

CHAPTER TWENTY

After Armageddon

They sat on the hill and pondered.

Rosalie's bones ached. Her head throbbed. This had to be the worst day of her life. Next to her, Chrystal was sobbing softly. Even Daphne looked at loose ends.

"I was his sweet chrysanthemum," Chrystal blurted out brokenly. "He sent me one every year on my birthday. . . ."

"One what?" Rosalie asked, distractedly.

Chrystal looked up, red-eyed. "On my birthday, like clockwork, I'd get this one beautiful chrysanthemum from him. . . ."

"He sent me a daffodil," said Daphne, in a strangled voice.

"And me, a rose," Rosalie said, tears burning in her eyes.

"A real botanical garden," said Iris, standing up and brushing herself off. "I say we kill the bastard. String him up by the balls in the public square. All in favor, say aye. . . ."

There were murmurs, then silence.

Iris looked disbelieving. "Well, come on, girls! We've got to do *something*. . . ."

Still, no one said anything.

"He ruined our lives, for godsakes!" Iris continued.

"Not exactly ruined," said Chrystal, thoughtfully. "Maybe it seemed that way, at first. . . ."

"Yeh," agreed Violetta Trubenik. "It could have been worse. I mean, he could have given us stupid kids." She half-smiled and added smugly, "My Jeraldine has an IQ of 235. She's at Oxford on a Rhodes Scholarship!"

Lilah Hassad considered. "That's good," she said. "But my Jared got a four-year, all-expense-paid scholarship to Harvard, and he's only nine years old!"

"And my Juliet—" someone else began.

"I don't believe what I'm hearing!" Iris exploded. "He seduced us, each and every one of us! He impregnated us, each and every one of us! Are we going to let him get away with it?"

"Sit down, Iris," Rosalie said firmly. "There's a lot we have to deal with. Don't let's make it worse."

Reluctantly, Iris sat down. She began to wail. "How could he have done this—to us? To me?"

"It's not all his fault," Rosalie said. "After all, we were willing, weren't we?"

"*More* than willing," someone said.

"That's no lie," said Posy O'Toole.

Daisy Gabboulian stood up. There was the hint of a belly beneath her blouse. Shakily, she admitted, "I wanted to have his baby. In fact, I *still* want to have it. . . ."

Chrystal stood and embraced the girl protectively. "No one's judging you, Daisy," she said softly.

"Maybe our mistake was in not telling him," Daphne said.

"Well, we all wanted to *spare* him," Iris said, wistfully. "We were young. What did we know?"

"Maybe it's not too late for Daisy," Rosalie said. "Maybe it's not too late for any of us. . . ."

They looked at each other. "Then is it agreed?" Rosalie asked. "Tonight, after the dinner, we'll tell him what we should have told him long ago. We'll take out the pictures of the kids and show him his family . . ."

"Give him a chance to explain . . ."

". . . to make reparation . . ."

". . . to let him know the joys of fatherhood . . ."

Iris was shaking her head wildly. "No! No, ladies! You're doing it all wrong! I still think we should kill the bastard."

CHAPTER
TWENTY-ONE

Bloom

He didn't look as bad as he felt, he thought, gazing at himself in the mirror. At least the tux still fit. And he had all his own hair. And all his own teeth. Not bad for a fifty-four-year-old cocker.

He grinned. God, he felt lousy. Maybe it was something he'd eaten. Maybe it was all the lifting and packing. Maybe it was all the stress of leaving Windsor College after all these years.

He sighed. He was having second thoughts about becoming the first Philosophical Advisor to the President of the United States. He wondered what his father would have said.

"Advisor, adshmisor, vadya need it for, boychik?"

Bloom shook his head and smiled. A grocer's mentality. Well, at least his mother would appreciate this latest step on his path to immortality. He was happy that he had found it within himself to forgive her for coming between him and his beloved Estrella so long ago. He'd even forgiven his sister Rochelle.

He could hear Rochelle now, tattling in that high, whining voice of hers, "Ma! I saw him in the alley with the *bummerke,* the super's daughter! They were doing it!"

His mother's screams could be heard from one end of Flatbush Avenue to the other. "Ay, ay, ay, ay!" she'd shrieked, ripping at the flowered cotton of her housedress. *"Gutt in himmel! A shondeh! A scandale! I'll kill the rotten kid!"*

She may as well have. She'd shipped him off to Princeton three weeks early. When he returned for Rosh Hashanah in the fall, Estrella was gone. The new super, Stanislaw Woldjiwicz, had never even heard of the DeSouzas. Or so he claimed. None of the neighbors were talking, either. It was as though his beloved Estrella had never even existed.

He glanced once more into the mirror and sighed again. Tonight he must make an effort to put Estrella DeSouza out of his thoughts once and for all. It wasn't going to be easy.

It never was.

He fumbled with his bow tie. *Damn!* He was never any good with these things. Where was Nora? She always helped him get ready.

He knocked gently on her dressing-room door. "Nora? You in there?"

The dressing-room door opened. He blinked. "Nora?" he gasped.

"Josiah, darling," she said softly. "I've been waiting for you."

He couldn't believe it. The change in her was astounding. More than astounding. It was miraculous.

When the dressing-room door had opened, he hadn't been prepared for the vision of loveliness that confronted him. Loveliness—and near nakedness. For thirty-five years, since her father's death, she'd been hiding herself under flannel nightgowns that buttoned up to her chin and black shroudlike dresses that made her look as though she lived in perpetual mourning. But now she was displaying her body in a pair of lacy black panties and a bra that did incredibly sensuous things to her breasts. Her hair, which she liked to wear swept severely back into a knot, now hung free and loose. Her dark eyes sparkled with mischief.

He caught a whiff of her perfume and the room spun.

"Nora," he managed to say. "What—"

She put a finger to his lips and led him to the bed.

"Josiah," she said, huskily, quickly unzipping his fly. "It's been so long. . . ."

"Nora," he groaned, wondering what miracle had brought about this stunning transformation. "Nora," he repeated. "My sweet, sweet nasturtium . . ."

They did things he'd only read about in cheap novels. Again and again he entered her, reveling in her moist, hot welcome. His tux lay in a crumpled heap on the floor. But who cared?

"Give it to me, big boy," she begged in a sultry voice reminiscent of her Amsterdam days. *"Do it to me!"*

He did it to her on the bed.

He did it to her standing up against the closet door.

He did it to her in the closet.

He did it to her in the bathroom while she sat on the edge of the sink, her legs snugly wrapped around his hips.

Was this the woman he'd labeled frigid? he wondered as she swung from the shower rod and invited him to put his tongue against her throbbing clit.

He wore out before she did. "No more, my sweet nasturtium," he begged. "Please, dearest . . ."

His tux looked as if a herd of elephants had slept on it. But they were already more than an hour late and there was no time to press it. Besides, who would be looking at him with the dazzling Nora at his side?

In her off-the-shoulder red satin gown, she was Athena and Aphrodite rolled into one. She'd adorned herself with the Haddock family jewels, a pair of long, diamond teardrops that dangled gracefully from her shell-like ears. A heart-shaped diamond brooch sparkled at her cleavage.

But why was she carrying such a large purse? he wondered.

CHAPTER TWENTY-TWO

Everything was going *exactly* as planned.

Men were such fools! They never questioned, they never analyzed. She felt almost sorry for Josiah, panting like the animal he was, obeying her every command.

Actually, the sex hadn't been quite as distasteful as she'd remembered. There was even a moment when she actually enjoyed it.

It was her gift to him. A proper send-off. Something for him to think about while he was rotting in purgatory.

They were going to miss cocktails. Good. She'd spared herself the hour of boring small talk with those insufferable Nobelists and their idiotic wives. To say nothing of Mama Bloom

and Rochelle. After tonight she'd never have to
see Mama and that loathsome Rochelle again.

Well, maybe *once* more. When they buried
him.

CHAPTER
TWENTY-THREE

Bluma

She was so nervous she could hardly button her
uniform. Everything was going wrong.

Claudette was positively rabid tonight. Partly,
Bluma suspected, because Claudette hadn't
planned on having to work. Tyrone, Claudette's
boyfriend, had tickets for jai alai in Milford. He
was furious with her because she couldn't go
with him.

"Why dey do dis to me?" Claudette raged,
banging pots and pans and slamming cabinet
doors. "It's not enuf I work de reg'lar shift in de
odder kitchen!"

The reason they needed Claudette on such
short notice in the Faculty Club kitchen was
this: Guido, the Faculty Club chef, had broken
his ankle and was confined to a wheelchair.

But that didn't stop Guido from trying to run

things. From his wheelchair he was shouting at all the kitchen help, and Claudette was running around like a chicken with its head cut off.

An *angry* chicken.

She thrust a tray at Bluma and instructed, "Hold it up like dis," she said, demonstrating. "You balance on de palm of yo' hand. Flat. Un-nerstan'?"

Bluma nodded. Her mouth was dry. It was one thing to score 1,600 combined on her SAT's. It was quite another to balance a heavily laden tray. She murmured a silent prayer to the Madonna that she would not spill a drop of soup on anybody's head.

"Dey fock me good," Claudette snarled under her breath. "Dey gonna lose my man for me. Dey gonna pay!" She slammed a cast-iron pan hard onto the range-top. In a loud voice she roared at Bluma, "You . . . ! You, work-study!"

Bluma stopped just as she was going through the swinging door. What now? she wondered.

"Your hair . . . !" Claudette roared. "Pull it back an' tie it!"

Bluma set the heavy tray carefully down on a counter. Claudette thrust a rubber band at her. Bluma did as she was told.

CHAPTER
TWENTY-FOUR

Dinner

It was almost more than Rosalie could bear. She felt as if she was being tugged in a thousand directions at once.

Since the cave debacle she'd hardly spoken a word to anyone. In the dorm room she and Chrystal had dressed in virtual silence, carefully avoiding each other's eyes.

She'd been tempted to pack her bag and go straight back to Beverly Hills. But no. She would see it through.

As though reading her mind, Chrystal sighed, "I don't know if I can do it. Tell him about Jace after all these years."

"It's not going to be easy. But we owe it to ourselves. And to the kids. And to Daisy . . ."

She sounded much more confident than she felt.

On the way down Bush Hill, Iris Ledbetter kept mumbling about how she wanted to see Bloom dead. But did she really? With Iris, it was hard to tell.

She tried to imagine how Bloom would react to the pictures of the kids. Was it too cruel? Or did he have a right to know?

God, she wished she had a cigarette. She'd stopped smoking ten years ago, but at this moment there was nothing she wanted more. Except, maybe, to discover that this whole day was nothing but a bad dream.

Once dressed, she and Chrystal made their way over to the Faculty Club. The sky above them was dark and starless. Even the moon had disappeared behind the clouds.

They heard footsteps behind them. Rosalie turned to see Daphne. "Are we really going to do it?" Daphne asked.

They had missed cocktails. Men in tuxes and women in long dresses were already seating themselves in the cherry-paneled dining room on the second floor of the Faculty Club.

Iris, already seated, looked ready to eat nails. She was wearing purple satin—a ruffled concoction complete with matching purple satin hat. A spray of velvet iris wound itself, vinelike, around the hat's broad brim.

When Rosalie, Chrystal, and Daphne approached the table, Iris glared at them. "You wimpy women! You let him walk all over you and all you're gonna do is shove some pictures in his face?" she hissed.

Rosalie closed her eyes. "Iris. Please. We've been over this a hundred times. If we kill him, we'll go to jail. Our way is going to be just as effective. . . ."

As they took their seats a voice behind Rosalie called, "Good evening, Mrs. Fine—"

Bluma stopped mid-sentence. "Mrs. Fineberg —are you okay?"

Was it that obvious? Rosalie wondered. She supposed it was. She'd been crying most of the afternoon. No amount of makeup could hide that fact. "I'm fine, Bluma, thank you," she lied.

At the front of the room was the dais. The long table was festooned with ferns and flower arrangements. Dignified men in black tie and bored-looking women sat waiting for the guest of honor to arrive.

Daphne asked what they were all thinking: "Where is he?"

Chrystal played with her salad. On the wall above the dais a banner declared "Farewell and *Bon Chance,* Dear Philosophical Advisor!" in yellow and pink, Windsor's colors.

She'd managed to take one bite of salad before Rosalie's friend reached in front of her and took the plate away. Well, let her. She couldn't eat, anyway. She could hardly breathe, in fact. She supposed she was in shock. And for good reason.

Suddenly there was a hush. And then a smattering of applause. Then the applause swelled to an ovation. Shouts of "Hear! Hear!" could be heard. Soon everyone was standing for a better look.

Daphne inhaled sharply as she caught a glimpse of the familiar red hair. Her heart raced. Ten years had only made him more handsome!

Chrystal's whole body was tingling at the sight of him. Was he looking at her? Did he see her? Her and only her?

Rosalie could barely stand. To be in the same room with him again! To breathe the same air! Where was the anger, the hurt, she'd felt only moments ago? Gone, at the mere sight of him. . . .

He smiled. All over the room, hearts were mending.

"Ladies and gentlemen," a voice boomed into the microphone. "It is my extreme pleasure to introduce our distinguished and revered guest of honor tonight, Dr. Josiah Mendelsohn Bloom!"

The room vibrated with applause.

Iris Ledbetter, hat askew, hoisted the ruffled

skirt of her purple satin dress to her thighs and climbed up on her chair. Applauding wildly, tears shining in her eyes, she screamed out, "Bravo! Bravo, Bloom!"

CHAPTER
TWENTY-FIVE

The Grand Finale

Was he dreaming? Bloom wondered. Was his mind playing tricks on him? Who were all those women cheering for him?

He could have sworn he saw Daisy Gabboulian. But no. She was safely at home. He squinted. In his rush he'd forgotten his glasses.

Seated on the dais to his right and to his left were his colleagues from Windsor, Senator Frimwick, and their wives. Out front he could see his fellow Nobelists—Saul, Jonas, Henry K., and, of course, Max Miller. (And there was Max's wife, Bliss, a truly delicious shiksa!)

And over there in the corner were Mama and

Rochelle, smiling up at him with undisguised pride.

But who were those women?

He made a courtly bow and cleared his throat. "My friends," he began. "My heart is filled with joy at seeing you gathered here tonight."

He waited for yet another round of applause to subside. "And now, my friends, let us enjoy our dinner and let the evening proceed."

A trio of musicians began to play light dinner music. He sat down next to Nora, who was smiling at him with a look of extreme happiness in her eyes. He took her hand and squeezed it.

After all these years, she had recovered completely.

Life was good.

Why was the service so abominably slow? Nora drummed her fingers on the table nervously. It had taken nearly an hour for the main course to be served. Now they were waiting endlessly for the dessert. She shifted uneasily. She had the uncomfortable feeling that things were starting to go wrong.

Why wasn't Josiah wearing his glasses? She wanted him to see his infernal girls, to know that she, Nora Haddock Bloom, knew all about them. Then and only then could she proceed.

Her hand strayed to her pocketbook, sitting heavily in her lap. All she had to do was reach down and take out Daddy's pearl-handled revolver and aim.

But not yet. First, they would have the baked Alaska. *If* it ever came! She had plotted so carefully to get Claudette to run the kitchen this evening, even going so far as paying that pompous Guido to feign a broken ankle!

So where was the baked Alaska?

Claudette was ready to kill. She stared at the sorry-looking mess that had started out to be baked Alaska but was now charred meringue, melted ice cream, and soggy cake.

She had waited *too* long. Getting even was one thing; losing her job was something else. She shrugged. Well, it was too late now to cry over melted Alaska.

"We can't keep 'em waitin' no longer," she muttered. *"Bluma!* Bring it out! Now!" she commanded.

Bluma hoisted the tray, stacked with ten plates of the oozing mush, and started through the swinging door. She would never understand a' woman like Claudette. This morning, at the Elias Windsor Hall and Dining Facility breakfast, Claudette had them working double time. Tonight she was making them move in slow motion, telling everyone to take their sweet time with the food.

As she entered the dining room she heard a soft ping. The rubber band! Her hair cascaded

down past her shoulders. She hoped Claudette
hadn't seen.

Madre mia, she thought. What else could possibly go wrong tonight?

Bloom thought Senator Frimwick had been
right to start the speeches while dessert was being served. For the last hour and a half he'd been
aware of people checking their watches, wondering, as he himself was, when the speeches
would finally begin.

"And now, ladies and gentlemen," the senator was saying, "the moment we've all been
waiting for has arrived. I present to you, once
more, our esteemed and revered colleague, the
first Philosophical Advisor to the President of
the United States of America, Dr. Josiah Mendelsohn Bloom!"

The applause was deafening. It was going on
and on. There were tears in his eyes. He lifted
his left arm to motion for silence, and felt an odd
tingly sensation.

He stood there, conscious of all their eyes
upon him.

"My dearest friends, how good of you to join
me here this evening. . . ."

He scanned the room. Damn, he wished he
had his glasses. *Who were those women?* Did he
know them? He thought he did.

"Leaving Windsor is probably the hardest
thing I'll ever have to do," he heard himself say.

Something was happening to the light. It was almost as if a mist was covering the room. He stared at the women. He *did* know them! At least one of them. The blonde. It was—could it be? *Yes!* Daphne Andrews! He grasped the lectern with both hands to steady himself. "Windsor has been my home for the past thirty-five years and . . ."

And next to Daphne—no, it couldn't be . . . *but it was!* Chrystal O'Neill! How he had loved her! Almost as much as he had loved Rosalie Samotsky, who—who was, miraculously, sitting next to Chrystal!

Was he seeing things? Was he hallucinating? He forced himself to go on. "Parting is such sweet roses," he heard himself say.

A small gasp escaped from someone seated in the audience.

"I mean—I mean, I mean—" he stammered, "parting is such sweet . . ." His eye caught a flash of purple satin. *"Iris!"* Now the lectern was tilting. He could feel beads of perspiration on his neck.

He tried to speak, but the heaviness that had lain in his chest all day had now risen to his throat. His lips moved, but no words were coming through.

From a great distance someone asked, "Dr. Bloom? Are you able to go on?"

He waved the intrusion away. Foolish question! Of course he was able to go on.

He gripped the lectern even tighter. Beneath his feet the floor was evaporating. He was beginning to float.

Suddenly he could see them all so clearly! Someone had gathered his flowers, brought them together into a loving bouquet. Just for him. What a wonderful thing to do!

Instinctively, he reached out to them. How he wanted to touch them, to caress them, to take them into his arms once again.

They had given him so much, these women. So much love. So much beauty. Love and beauty. The eternal blessings of the human spirit . . .

Someone moved behind him now. Someone with long, black, *wild* hair. The waitress? No. *Not* the waitress.

He turned. She was as beautiful as ever, his beloved Estrella. He stared in disbelief. How marvelous she looked! Exactly the way she'd looked all those years ago, when she'd taught him the meaning of love. . . .

He reached out to her. *"Estrella!"* he whispered. He'd meant to shout it. *"Estrella!"* he tried again as he fell into the light, grabbing on to her.

"Estrella, Estrella, my heart . . ." he called as the light grew brighter and brighter, blinding him forever in its relentless brilliance.

CHAPTER TWENTY-SIX

Aftermath

The Tinguely *Eagle*
May 26, 1988
SPECIAL EDITION
Catastrophe Strikes at Windsor College
Banquet by Dorothy Pingouin
Last night, before a packed banquet hall in
the Faculty Club of Windsor College, Tin-
guely's most famous and beloved resident,
Professor Josiah Mendelsohn Bloom, twice
winner of the Nobel Prize, was felled by a
massive coronary. All attempts at resuscita-
tion proved futile.

After thirty-five years of meritorious service as head of the Philosophy Department at
the College, Dr. Bloom was planning to assume the position of Philosophical Advisor to
the President of the United States.

Senator Alton Frimwick, the Republican

Senator from South Cranbury, who was sitting
on the dais with Dr. Bloom when he was
stricken, declared his profound sorrow and
shock. "This is indeed a great loss to our country and to the world at large. Dr. Bloom was a
man of outstanding ability. We shall all miss
him greatly."

Ms. Bluma DeSouza, a work-study student
waitress, was the first to attempt cardiopul-
monary resuscitation on the fallen professor.

"It happened so fast," Ms. DeSouza said.
"Just when I was serving the melted Alaska
[sic], he fell and grabbed onto me."

Ms. DeSouza, who received her CPR train-
ing in her native Puerto Rico, is the niece of
Ernesto DeSouza of Tinguely. Ms. DeSouza,
visibly shaken, kept repeating, "It was the
strangest thing," but refused to say more.

Dr. Bloom is survived by his wife, the former Nora Haddock; his mother, Bella Bloom
of Monticello, New York; a sister, Rochelle
Schwartz, also of Monticello, New York; and
two nieces. Dr. and Mrs. Bloom had no children.

(See Page 14 for excerpts from Dr. Bloom's
works.)

PART THREE
What Goes 'Round Comes 'Round

CHAPTER
TWENTY-SEVEN

Endings

Rosalie had never seen such chaos. Secret Service men were everywhere. The press too. Television cameras. Reporters. Miscellaneous paparazzi. Not to mention the entire population of Tinguely, Connecticut.

"It's a three-ring circus," she said to Chrystal as they followed the cordoned-off path that led to Andrews Chapel. "What do you think he would have said?"

Chrystal shrugged. "Who knows anymore?" she sniffled, fishing in her purse for yet another tissue. "Did we really know what he liked?"

Rosalie shook her head. "I still can't believe it," she said. "One minute, he was alive, and the next minute, he was—"

"Don't say it," Daphne said. "This can't be happening."

As they approached the chapel steps a photographer jumped out from behind a bush of rhododendrons and pushed his camera into Daphne's face.

"Hey, Scrumptious!" he called. "How well did you know the old guy?"

Without answering, Daphne covered her face with her hands and rushed past him into the chapel.

The organ was playing Felix Mendelssohn's "Funeral Fugue in G Minor." The air was heavy with the smell of flowers.

In the first pew they saw a catatonic Nora Bloom. She was dressed in black from head to toe. She sat unmoving, her eyes fixed on Bloom's casket.

"Poor woman," said Rosalie as they slid into their seats in the third pew.

"Yes, poor Nora." Chrystal nodded. Almost as a second thought, she asked, "Do you think she ever knew about us?"

"Of course not," said Daphne. "How could she?"

They sat in silence, waiting for the chapel to fill and the eulogies to begin. Rosalie looked around. Over there, in the corner, sat the same people who'd been on the dais with Bloom last night. She recognized most of the faces. After all, they were some of the most well-known, well-respected people in the world.

She closed her eyes for a moment. They hadn't been able to show him the pictures of the kids after all. He died believing that he was childless. The irony was almost too much. . . .

She became aware of a keening wail. She opened her eyes to see Nora Bloom standing in the front pew. "How could you do this to me, Josiah? How could you betray me like this?" she raved. She ran to the casket and pounded angrily on it with her fists.

"Why did you die so soon?" Nora wailed, climbing on the casket, still pounding. "You weren't supposed to die yet! Not yet! Later! Later!"

A camera flashed as William Bender Cavendish, the president of the college, aided by Senator Frimwick and Max Miller (one of the Nobelists), grabbed Nora and carried her back to her pew.

The widow's wails were drowned out seconds later by the rasping whirr of a helicopter landing on the Andrews Chapel lawn.

Everywhere the Secret Service men sprang into action. They tapped their earphones, synchronized their watches, nodded to themselves and to each other.

The President of the United States of America had arrived!

People shifted expectantly in their pews, craning their necks for a better view of the

Chief of State, who had taken the time from his busy schedule to pay his last respects to the Philosophical Advisor-to-be, who, alas, would never be.

CHAPTER
TWENTY-EIGHT

Vinnie

God, he could use a six-pack. God, he needed a game to watch. But baseball had been pre-empted for this stupid funeral thing. Big deal! Some big-shot professor croaks and there goes the afternoon!

He hunkered down into his end of the couch and punched the buttons on the remote.

Funeral. *Click.* Funeral. *Click.* Lizards humping on a rock in some desert. *Click!* Well, he knew when he was licked. He settled down and watched the funeral.

He took a gulp of diet soda and forced it down. Staying on the wagon was going to be tougher than he thought. Still, he'd made the promise to himself. . . . He was going to pull himself together once and for all, no buts about it.

Jace was on the phone in the kitchen. He must

have finally gotten through to that history teacher of his with the bum car. Vinnie smiled. Leave it to Jace to drum up business for his old man.

Theresa and the twins were still at church with Chrystal's mom. He looked at his watch. He had maybe forty minutes to himself. He squinted at the screen. Some hot babe in a white dress was running past the camera like she didn't want to be seen. And then—he sat up. Holy . . . !

"Jace!" he yelled. "Get in here! Quick! Your mom's on television . . . !"

He couldn't believe his eyes. There she was. His Chrystal! What was she doing on television? Just then the camera switched to some announcer. For the first time, Vinnie listened.

"And so, ladies and gentlemen, we wait here on the campus of Windsor College in beautiful Tinguely, Connecticut, for the arrival of the President of the United States. . . ."

Vinnie sat up straighter. "Windsor? For cryin' out loud! The funeral is at Windsor!" He clapped his hand to the side of his head. The big shot! He was the one they were giving that dinner for! "Malatesta!" he muttered to himself. "Try puttin' two an' two together!"

Last night, when Chrystal had called, he could hardly understand what she was saying. For one thing, it was a lousy connection. For another, he was so happy to hear her voice, he didn't even listen to what she was saying. Something about somebody dying . . . one of her old teachers or something. How was he to know the guy was important enough for the President to show up at his funeral?

Jace came bounding into the room. "Where?" he yelled excitedly.

"Oh, too late," Vinnie said. "You missed her."

"You sure it was her?"

"Sure I'm sure. I know your mother when I see her."

The two of them sat wordlessly in front of the TV, hoping to catch another glimpse of Chrystal. No luck. Instead, all they saw were pictures of this guy Bloom shaking hands with everyone who was anyone in the whole damn world.

The guy wasn't much to look at. A schnozz like Durante's. Hair like red Brillo. A phony baloney smile.

"Mom had him, Dad," Jace said.

Vinnie, startled, said, "Huh?"

Jace nodded. "Yeah, Dad," the boy said calmly. "He was her philosophy professor. She gave me one of his books. Book One of the *History of American Thought*. A bit on the wordy side, if you ask me." Jace paused and peered at him. Shyly, he asked, "Didn't she ever tell you about him?"

No. Goddammit, she hadn't. In fact, Chrystal never told him anything about her college days.

But maybe it wasn't all her fault. Maybe he never gave her a chance.

When she called last night he'd tried to tell her how much he missed her, that he would do right by her from now on. No more lying around watching TV, no more guzzling beer. But, somehow, the words just wouldn't come. And when she'd mentioned she'd be staying at Windsor an extra day for the funeral, he'd gotten pissed.

"Geez, Chrystal," he'd pouted. "The kids are gonna be disappointed." He'd said *the kids.* Why didn't he tell her *he* was gonna be disappointed?

She'd said something he didn't hear and hung up.

He didn't even get a chance to tell her about the letter that had come for her from New York. From the publisher. But maybe he was doing her a favor. Suppose the letter was another rejection? He remembered the last time she'd gotten a rejection. She'd locked herself in the bathroom and cried for hours. She hadn't even made them dinner that night.

But suppose it *wasn't* a rejection this time? His stomach tightened. Suppose someone really wanted to publish that book of hers? The book she'd never let him see, by the way. And which he suspected was all about the guy that had knocked her up. Suppose she got famous? Suppose she got rich? It happened sometimes. This was America, the land of golden opportunity, after all.

If Chrystal got rich and famous from that book of hers, would she want to stay married to a one-footed, lazy, good-for-nothing *chooch?*

He shook his head.

Jace was yammering on about something. Something about a Mr. Shrubsole, who was coming over in a few minutes to have his alternator looked at.

CHAPTER
TWENTY-NINE

Milton

He didn't want to go. On the other hand, he did. Curiosity impelled him. Still, he had no right to insinuate himself into her life. Not after she'd told him, plain and simple, that she could never see him again.

"It's over," she'd said that last time they were together. "I don't like sneaking around like this, like a cheap—"

He wouldn't let her finish. "Shhh," he said, touching his finger to her lips. "There's nothing cheap about you, Chrystal, my darling. I love you. I want to marry you. There's nothing dishonest about our seeing each other."

She'd looked into his eyes for a long time. And then she'd said, "Milton. I'm already married. I'm committing adultery. It's a sin."

He threw up his hands and stared at the ceiling. "I'll tell you what the real sin is! You're wasting your life with a bum! A lazy, no-good bum!"

"He's still my husband," she countered.

And so, reluctantly, they'd said good-bye.

That was a month ago, and he hadn't been able to get her out of his mind since. Especially today. The television was filled with news of Windsor College and the death of Josiah Mendelsohn Bloom. She'd mentioned Bloom several times. Milton sensed that the man had some sort of hold over her. Chrystal had read everything Bloom ever wrote. She quoted whole paragraphs from his books. She could recite his lectures verbatim fourteen years after graduation!

Well, now Bloom was dead. Chrystal was probably devastated. Milton wished he could put his arm around her and let her cry on his shoulder.

Then fate took over. The phone rang and he heard Jace Malatesta's voice. Why was Chrystal's son calling him? Had something happened to her? Had Jace found out about them?

But no. Jace was talking cars.

"Mr. Shrubsole? You still need work on that alternator?"

Milton swallowed. "My car? Sure. That stupid alternator's been giving me trouble for weeks. . . ."

"Well, in case you haven't heard, my pop is a great mechanic. He just fixed our old Chevy and it's like new. He has some free time this afternoon. You want to bring your car over and let him have a look?"

Milton hesitated. He hadn't initiated this opportunity to finally meet the famous Vinnie. It had fallen like a ripe plum into his palm. For nearly a year he'd been hearing about this slob who couldn't lift himself off the couch long enough to find a job. The bum let his wife support him, for crying out loud! He'd lay even money that the guy knew zilch about cars. But what did he have to lose? The old Buick was a goner anyway.

To Jace he said, "Well, I don't know. It's Sunday. Aren't your folks going out for dinner or something?" His own cleverness astounded him, saying "folks" like that, as if he didn't know that Chrystal was up at Windsor for the weekend.

"No, my mom's not even home, and my dad has plenty of time."

I bet he does, thought Milton.

"So what do you say, Mr. S.?"

"I say yes," Milton said. "I'll be right over."

CHAPTER THIRTY

Kermit

He'd been making passionate love to her, driving her insane with wanting him. "Please, please . . . now! Now Kermit, I want it—I want you—oh, God . . . !"

He drove himself into her like a sledgehammer, pounding, thrusting, heaving, meeting her pfumpf for pfumpf. . . .

Pfumpf for pfumpf? He opened his eyes and found himself fucking the pillow. "Jesus," he muttered as disappointment rose within him. The dream had been so vivid! So real! In it Rosalie had never looked more beautiful. How he missed her!

He looked at the clock. Nearly midnight. Through the open window he saw a sliver of moon in the starry sky. It must be nearly three in the morning in Connecticut.

She was probably asleep.

Yes, but was she alone?

He wouldn't really blame her if she wasn't. After all, things hadn't been so great between them for months. And whose fault was it but his?

Oy. He should never have started with that Biffy Barclay in the first place. In the second place, he should have dropped *Yesterday's News* like a hot potato before he got burned.

Should have, should have. His life was nothing but should-haves.

The phone rang suddenly, scaring the bejeezus out of him. He moved toward it and was reminded none too gently that his back was not yet 100 percent. He put the receiver to his ear and barked out a hello.

She sounded like he felt. Worse. Like she'd been crying. "Rosalie? What's wrong, honey?"

"Kermit, Bloom is dead," she blubbered.

Bloom? Who the hell was Bloom? A director? An agent? A writer?

Then he remembered. Bloom was the guy who was leaving Windsor College to go work in Washington. The guy from the farewell banquet. He was the reason Rosalie had gone East in the first place.

"Rosalie, baby, what can I say? I'm devastated."

She went on. "Kermit, one minute he was up there talking and the next he was on the floor flat on his back. . . ."

Kermit knew from flat on his back. But did

Rosalie care that he spent the last day and a half on the floor? Should he tell her? Not only about his back, but how he felt about her, how he loved her, how he wished she was here beside him?

"Rosalie . . ." he started, but she was crying.

And then she said, "Kermit, I may be staying out here a little longer. There's the funeral, and who knows what . . ."

What could he say to that?

"Sure, sure, babe, I understand."

But he didn't understand. Not really.

CHAPTER THIRTY-ONE

Sidney

He was still trembling when he got out of the subway at Pelham Parkway. What had possessed him to lend Daphne his Land Rover in the first place? Okay, so he loved her. But a lot of guys loved women without lending them their cars! But then, how could he know what was going to happen?

When the first kid had sidled up to him on the train, glaring, standing right in front of him even though the car was nearly empty, he hadn't thought too much of it. He'd simply dug into his pocket and handed over a five-dollar bill. But then, as if out of nowhere, three more kids had materialized, hovering menacingly. He forced himself to meet their eyes—wild, crazy, do-anything eyes—and reached back into his pocket. Wordlessly, he gave them the twenty, the fifty, and both hundreds. Finally, he surrendered his wallet.

Damn! Sid thought. He should have taken a cab. But Pelham Parkway was a helluva long ride from his office on Park Avenue. . . .

The hoodlums were staring at him. He felt dizzy, light-headed. And then he noticed that one of them was holding a screwdriver. His heart lurched. Never had he known such raw terror, not even that time when he was a resident and had to treat the ax murderer at Bellevue.

"T'anks, mistuh." The kid holding the screwdriver smiled.

"You're welcome," Sid rasped. He held his breath as the punk leaned over. He closed his eyes and prayed it would be quick.

And then he heard the slow squeak of screws being turned. He opened his eyes. The boy was calmly unscrewing the advertising placard behind him. It was a brand-new shiny poster of a smiling Vanna White. "What will Vanna wear tonight?" the ad wanted to know.

The boy rolled up the poster and smiled to his friends. The smiles turned to laughter. The train screeched to a stop. One of them winked. "So long, suckuh," he said, joining his friends on the platform.

Sid ran all the way to his mother's building. When he got there she refused to buzz him inside unless he told her the secret password.

"But, Ma," he protested. "It's me! Sidney Funt! Your son!"

In a wry voice he knew only too well, she said, "How do I know? My Sidney always calls before he visits. And he doesn't visit so often. So please, the password."

What the hell was the damn password? She kept changing it every five minutes. Last time it was "grandchildren." Before that it was "bride." Before that, "money in the bank." As in "Why don't you have money in the bank so you can take a bride and give me grandchildren?"

"Grandchildren?" Sidney said hopefully.

"Wrong!" his mother sang out. "That was last time! What's the new one?"

He searched his brain. He couldn't really blame her for being cautious. Not after his subway experience. But he was her son, for God's sake! There had to be a limit to how cautious a mother was entitled to be.

"I don't know the new one, Ma," he admitted.

"Well," she said, "if you came more often, you'd know it."

There was a long pause. He thought they were finished with this kind of manipulative monkey business. How long was she going to go on punishing him for not becoming a plastic surgeon? Or at least making a million dollars on Wall Street? Or even being a TV producer like his cousin Allen?

And then he had an idea.

"Come to the window," he said. "Take a look. *See* if it's me."

Reluctantly, she agreed.

Sidney ran from the vestibule around the corner. He looked up. His mother, seven stories above him, looked down.

He ran inside again and reached the door just before it stopped buzzing.

She took one look and said, "My God, Sidney, you're so pale! You're not eating right! It's all those crazy people you see! They're making you sick!"

"I'm fine," he insisted. "Really, Ma." He'd already decided not to tell her about the subway incident. It would only upset her. Besides, he'd come here today to tell her something that would make her very happy. He'd tell her what she'd been waiting her whole life to hear—that he, Sidney Funt, M.D., was in love and ready to settle down.

"Sit down, Ma," he said.

She sat down. "Sidney, if it's bad news, I don't wanta know."

Sidney smiled. "It's good news, Ma. I've met her. I've met the woman I'm going to marry."

His mother didn't move. He thought at first that she hadn't heard. But then she put her hand to her ample bosom and looked up at him. "Marry?" she said, almost in a whisper. "Don't joke with me, Sidney. I'm an old woman."

He shook his head. "I'm not joking. She's wonderful, Ma. You'll love her."

Suddenly they became aware of the noise coming from the television set in the living room. Since his father died three years ago, his mother kept the television set on day and night to keep her company. Maybe she needed a companion. Maybe he'd get her a puppy. Or better yet, when he and Daphne were settled and in their own place, maybe they'd ask his mother to come live with them.

"Wait," his mother said, going into the living room to lower the sound. Sid glanced at the TV screen. *There she was! "There she is!"* he yelled.

His mother looked. Barbara Walters's face filled the screen. "As we wait for the awwival of the Pwesident of the United States of Amewica—"

"You're marrying Barbara Walters!" his mother exclaimed, her eyes wide as saucers.

Sidney shook his head. His fingers were on the knobs now, frantically switching channels. On Channel 2 he saw the Windsor College campus and a shot of a group of women entering a chapel. There she was again. Daphne. Dressed in white and protecting herself from an intruding camera. "There she is again, Ma," he said. "The one in white."

"That's not Barbara," his mother said with a trace of disappointment.

"Of course not," said Sidney. "Her name is

Daphne Banks. She's the Scrumptious Yogurt Girl."

His mother looked confused. "But Barbara's such a nice girl. . . ."

"Stop already with Barbara," Sidney said, his attention focusing on the TV screen. What was going on? he wondered. On Channel 2 a somber Dan Rather gave him the answer.

"Josiah Mendelsohn Bloom, possibly one of the greatest philosophers of our era, died suddenly last night at a banquet held in his honor at Windsor College in Tinguely, Connecticut. . . ."

"That's where she is!" Sid shouted.

"A college girl, Sidney?" His mother frowned.

Sid sank down into the plastic-coated depths of his mother's armchair. *Bloom.* Hadn't Daphne mentioned him a couple of times? Wasn't he her professor? He closed his eyes and remembered the look on her face when she spoke about him. Awe. Reverence. Love? he wondered now. Was Bloom the one? The primary fidelity guy? The source of her present inability to reach orgasm?

He had to go to her. If Daphne *ever* needed him, Sidney Funt, M.D., it would be now!

But how was he going to get to Tinguely? Daphne had his car.

Well, he would rent a car.

Then he remembered. He had given his wallet and every last dollar in it to those punks on the subway. His credit cards too.

Maybe Reinisch! Reinisch had an old Volvo that he cherished. But maybe, just this once, he would be willing to part with it. After all, this was an emergency.

He stood up and bolted for the door. "Gotta go, Ma," he said.

"But—but you just got here! You call this a visit? And what about your girl?"

"It's her I gotta go to," he said urgently. Then he paused. "Uh . . . Ma . . . I need a favor. . . ."

"Anything, Sidney. What have I ever denied you?"

"I need cab money, Ma."

She rolled her eyes to the ceiling. "A psychiatrist he had to be," she said to the ceiling. "He couldn't be a plastic surgeon and make some money for a change?" She sighed.

"Just a twenty, Ma. I'll pay you back next week. I promise."

She reached inside her brassiere and pulled out a roll of bills. She peeled off two twenties and put them in his hand. "Here's a little extra," she said. "Buy yourself lunch."

CHAPTER THIRTY-TWO

The Long Road Home

Chrystal looked into the rearview mirror and saw Andrews Chapel shrink into the sunset. Determinedly, she swung the Dodge onto the expressway. But the road kept blurring.

She would never return to Windsor College. It was a part of her life that was over. The shock of the past three days was still with her. She could hardly think. Her brain reeled. First, the terrible revelation that she was not Bloom's *only* love. And then, before she could sort out that mess, had come his death.

She pressed harder on the accelerator.

The whole funeral had seemed surreal. The President's speech, the flowers, the Secret Service men, the whole circuslike atmosphere. Ultimately, she had forced herself to view him one last time.

Gazing down at him in the open casket, she had forgiven him utterly. He looked so innocent lying there like that. In life, too, Bloom had been an innocent, caught up by circumstances. He had meant them no harm. He had felt only love for them all. She was sure of it.

She drove past a McDonald's and realized that she had hardly eaten all weekend. She pulled into the parking lot and switched off the ignition. She looked at herself in the rearview mirror. She looked like a waif, which, she supposed, she was . . . in a way. After so many years of clinging to the memory of Bloom, she was suddenly set adrift. Directionless. Which way should she go now?

Milton Shrubsole was the wrong way, that she knew. He was a decent, good man, but there was really no place for him in her life. She had no roots with Milton.

With Vinnie, at least, she had roots.

But were roots enough?

Rosalie leaned back against the seat and closed her eyes. The constant drone of the engines soothed her abused psyche. The seats in coach were smaller, closer together than in first class, but she'd been lucky to get a seat at all. She had, of course, canceled her reservation to return to L.A. earlier in the day. But after the funeral she couldn't wait to leave Windsor.

She didn't care if she never saw the campus again.

The funeral had gone on forever, it seemed. Too many eulogies, too many empty words. The Bloom all those important men remembered was not the man she had loved so completely all these years.

How could she have been so duped?

She knew how. She'd been young. Young and hungry for love. Bloom had been brilliant, and powerful, and his need for her had overwhelmed her.

The plane hit a bump and her eyes flew open. The blonde to her left gasped. "Oh, God," she whined. "I hope we don't crash!"

Rosalie looked at her sympathetically. The girl was young—about twenty. Probably on her way to Hollywood to become a movie star. "Don't worry about it," Rosalie told her. "Just a little turbulence."

The girl gave her a weak smile. "I'm on my way to live with my cousin in Santa Monica. She has a job at Universal. She says they're always looking for new faces. . . ."

Rosalie summoned the semblance of a smile. "Good luck," she said, hoping her sarcasm didn't show. She felt sorry for the girl.

In the window seat, to Rosalie's right, sat an obviously pregnant young woman who stared interminably into the blackness of the sky. Rosalie glanced at the woman's left hand. No ring.

It was as though she was surrounded by fragments of her own past, a lopsided mosaic of memories that had no center.

Well, at least she was going home. But where was home now that Bloom was dead?

Was it with Kermit? She was almost certain he was having an affair. How else to explain those red silk bikini briefs and his inability to get it up with her?

And yet, when she'd called him yesterday, he'd sounded so happy to hear from her. Although he didn't say it, she had the feeling that he missed her. Perhaps he did. But more to the point, did she miss him?

He was a good father to Josie. But Josie was almost grown. In another year she would be on her way to college. Then there would be just the two of them. Would they be able to make it as a couple?

They would both have to change. For her part, Bloom—or the illusion of Bloom—had prevented her from loving Kermit fully. Perhaps Kermit had sensed that. She remembered how wounded he'd looked every year when her birthday rose had arrived. The first few times he'd been curious about who had sent her the rose. Naturally, she'd never told him.

And then he'd stopped asking. But the hurt in his eyes never left.

* * *

Daphne was too exhausted to get mad all over again at the stupid slowness of Sid's car. Besides, she was grateful now for the extra time it gave her to think.

What a fool she'd been, believing in Bloom. All those times he'd said he loved her and only her. She'd never suspected there was another. *Thirty-four others!*

Well, at least she had Josh.

She yawned and glanced in the rearview mirror. Her bones ached. Her heart was sore with the beating it had taken. She felt as if she'd been driving for hours. The luminous dial on the dashboard said 4 A.M. Still, she was glad she hadn't stayed another night at Windsor.

Absently, she switched on the radio. Ray Charles's raspy voice crooned, "I can't stop loving you . . ." She hummed along.

She supposed she would never stop loving Bloom. That was the irony. Still, it would be different. Now she was free of illusions. In a crazy way, Bloom's death had released her.

She noticed that the sky was beginning to lighten. For nearly an hour she hadn't seen another car on the road. But now, when she glanced in the mirror, she saw headlights.

What idiot was out driving at this hour?

CHAPTER
THIRTY-THREE

New
Beginnings

It was after midnight when Chrystal pulled her brother Sean's Dodge into the driveway.

She rubbed her eyes and squinted at the house. There was a light on in their bedroom window! A flash of terror gripped her. Vinnie always fell asleep on the couch in the living room. So why was there a light on upstairs?

Could he be sick? Maybe one of the kids?

She got out of the car and had another shock. Ahead of her in the driveway was their old Chevy. And another car. *Milton's car!*

Trembling, she headed for the front door. She was halfway there when the porch light went on. The door opened. Someone was standing there.

"Chrys? Honey? That you?"

"Vinnie?" she whispered.

He was coming toward her. Slowly. Haltingly. *Not hopping*. Vinnie was walking!

Was she dreaming? Had she fallen asleep on the road and died?

"Chrystal, babe," Vinnie said, nearing her. "I was gettin' worried. You all right?"

She looked down. He was wearing pajamas. From the bottom of his left leg, where there should have been nothing, a slipper protruded!

"Vinnie?" she gasped. "You're walking!"

He smiled. "This is only the beginnin', babe," he said, drawing her into his arms. He smelled of talc and soap and something else. Motor oil?

"I missed ya so much, Chrystal," Vinnie said, his lips finding hers.

In his arms she felt the weight of the past few days—*years*—slip from her shoulders. She closed her eyes. "Vinnie," she sighed, "I'm so happy to be home."

It was 6 A.M. Los Angeles time, but the gray Fineberg Films limo was waiting. Rosalie had no idea how Kermit knew what flight she was taking, but she wasn't going to question it. She was delirious with fatigue and happy that Kermit had thought to send a driver.

As she neared the limo the back door sprang

open. She peered inside. "Kermit?" she asked, incredulously.

He extended his hand and pulled her in alongside him.

"Welcome home, sweetheart," he said, taking her into his arms.

"But—" she began.

He silenced her with a kiss. His lips were warm and gentle, as if he'd been waiting a long time for this. "Don't ever leave me again," he said, huskily. "Promise me."

"I promise," she heard herself say.

She meant it. "I'll never leave you, Kermit," she said, her eyes brimming. "I've come home to stay."

The headlights of the car behind Daphne grew larger and larger. The jerk had his brights on and was flashing them at her. What did he expect her to do? She was already in the slow lane and there was nobody else on the road!

Instinctively, she pushed down on the accelerator. A lot of good that did! The Rover hardly noticed.

And then she heard it. Her name.

"Daphne! Daphne! Pull over!"

Was she dreaming? How could this stranger in the old Volvo know her name? Then she heard it again.

"Daphne, I love you!"

She knew a moment of panic. Suppose it was

some lunatic out to find a vulnerable woman alone on the road at night? Suppose he wanted to commit heinous acts?

But how would he know her name?

The Volvo drew up alongside her in the left lane. The man was gesturing wildly for her to roll down her window. She did.

"Daphne!" he shrieked. "It's me! Sidney Funt, M.D.! The man you're going to marry!"

EPILOGUE
One Year Later

Rosalie and Kermit

She was shaking. She hadn't had such an attack of nerves since Josie got the acceptance from Harvard.

Now she was all thumbs as she fumbled with the diamond earrings Kermit had presented to her on her birthday just a few days ago. It had been a happy birthday from start to finish. First the party at the Golden Ibis with half the movie colony in attendance. Then the post-midnight sail on Kermit's new yacht with just a few hundred of their closest friends.

Then, later, just the two of them together, making the kind of love that lasts.

The earrings had really stunned her. Two-carat perfect solitaires for each ear. "Perfect gems for my perfect Rosalie," he'd said with a smile.

"I love you, Kermit," she'd said, meaning every word.

At first she was wary of Kermit's new devotion to her. Ever since that morning at the airport he'd been a changed man. There was no more staring into space, no more distractions, no more red silk bikini briefs. Whatever fling he'd flung was obviously over.

When he began to open up to her about business, she knew he was back for good.

He was scrapping *Yesterday's News*, deep-sixing it forever. "I was a schmuck to take it on," he'd admitted. "Stupid not to have consulted you . . ."

It took courage to scrap a project in this town, and she respected him for it. They'd gone through a rough couple of months with the lawyers and the accountants, but they'd come through it.

And from the ashes of *Yesterday's News* had miraculously risen *Sweet Awakenings*.

It was serendipitous. Last July, Chrystal Malatesta had written a note announcing the publication of her book. It was a chatty note, full of hope and optimism:

When I got home from that awful weekend at Windsor, everything changed. Was it the same for you?

Vinnie had already started a new business! It's perfect for him—fixing cars—and it's doing quite well.

But the best part was the letter from the publisher that was sitting there waiting for me. They've bought Sweet Awakenings! I'm so excited, Rosalie. After all these years, things are finally starting to happen for me. . . .

The rest was history. Rosalie called Chrystal's publisher and requested the galleys. They arrived Air Express the next day. As her eyes flew over the pages she knew immediately that Chrystal's novel would be a best seller. Better— that a movie version of *Sweet Awakenings* would be solid gold.

The novel was, of course, autobiographical. It was about Bloom. But it was also about a young, innocent girl who fell in love with an irresistible older man and how their love affair changed her life.

Rosalie handed the galleys to Kermit. When he'd finished he'd looked up at her with an unreadable expression. "A good story, Rosalie," he said. And then he asked, "Is it your story, Rosalie?"

She wondered if this was the time to tell him everything. But what good would that do? So she said, "It's my story, it's Chrystal's story, it's every woman's story."

Kermit seemed satisfied. They bought the movie rights and production started almost immediately.

They'd wanted Michael Caine for the professor, but unfortunately he had other commitments. Instead, they cast Barron Heatter, who seemed perfect for the part.

They had a tougher time casting the part of the girl. They auditioned hundreds of eager starlets, including the blonde who'd sat next to her on the plane coming home from Windsor. But none of them seemed exactly right.

And then, late one night, while she was watching television—Kermit was already asleep in bed next to her—she'd seen the Scrumptious commercial. "Of course!" she'd screamed. "Why didn't I think of it before?"

Startled, Kermit woke up. "What . . . what . . . ?"

She pointed to the television screen. "Look! Quick!"

Kermit looked. "Yogurt? I hate yogurt!"

"No—the girl! That's Daphne!"

He watched, bleary-eyed, as the camera caressed Daphne's beautiful face. As she spooned the yogurt into her lovely mouth, the voice-over cooed, "Pure. Creamy. Yum. *Scrumptious!*"

They looked at each other.

"That's her! The girl!" said Kermit.

* * *

And now, nearly eight months later, *Sweet Awakenings* was premiering in key cities all around the country.

The bedroom door opened. Josie, resplendent in her new turquoise gown, poked her head in. "Hey, you guys, let's move it!" she said excitedly. She looked at Rosalie. "Mom, you look utterly rad, gnarly as hell."

Rosalie beamed. She was wearing a black silk sheath to set off the brilliance of the earrings Kermit had given her. Her hair was swept back into a French knot. The effect, Rosalie had to admit, was dazzling.

Kermit emerged from the dressing room.

"C'mon, Daddy," Josie urged. "Let's hurry. You can't be late for your own premiere!"

And so, arm in arm in arm, the three of them left the house. They were a real family at last, Rosalie knew. There were no more ghosts from her past to drive a wedge between them.

It was just them, together. The way it should be.

Chrystal and Vinnie

She had almost gone to the Hollywood premiere of *Sweet Awakenings,* but at the last minute she'd decided it would be better to stay home with Vinnie and the kids. There was so much to do, what with the new house and Vinnie's business and all.

The details were crowding her brain. Did they want Formica cabinets in the kitchen? Or oak? The staircase leading to her studio—should it be circular or traditional? The faucets in the two downstairs bathrooms and the three bathrooms upstairs—gold or silver? Or maybe brass and lucite?

It was all too much for Vinnie to handle alone. Especially since Malatesta Motors had expanded twice in the last six months. Poor Vinnie. He was so overworked. Even though he now had a staff of twenty under him, the customers still demanded his personal expertise.

And as if that wasn't enough, in another two weeks Jace would be graduating from Boonton Harbor High School—the youngest graduate in the history of the school!

Jace. How she would miss him when he went off to Princeton and the Institute for Advanced Studies in the fall. . . .

Idly, she settled back on the new modular sofa and, flanked by Theresa and Heather, pressed the remote for the new projection TV.

"This is *so* exciting, Mom!" Theresa said, snuggling against her.

"Yeah, Mom." Heather smiled. "I can't believe your book is actually a movie!"

To tell the truth, she could hardly believe it herself. When the book was accepted for publication last year, she had no idea it would turn out to be a blockbuster best-seller. Twenty weeks on *The New York Times* best-seller list so far! And that wonderful call from Rosalie, saying that Kermit was going to rush production of the movie version.

But what most confounded her were the endless articles that kept appearing week after week in magazines and newspapers.

Only last week there was that story in *FOLK* magazine. How did they manage to find her old

Windsor yearbook picture? But there it was, alongside Daphne's and Rosalie's. "Three Windsor Gals Make It Big!"

Funny how all the reporters asked the same questions: "Is *Sweet Awakenings* autobiographical?" "Is the older man in the book really the late Dr. Josiah Mendelsohn Bloom?"

Her answer was always the same. "It's all fiction. Every word is pure fiction. I write fiction."

They didn't believe her, but that was *their* problem.

Now, Casey Kasem's smiling face flashed on the TV screen. "Greetings from Hollywood, ladies and gentlemen," he began. "It seems every bright star in filmdom is here tonight to celebrate what will surely be the megahit of our generation, Fineberg Films's *Sweet Awakenings . . . !*"

Theresa jumped up and ran into the kitchen. "Jace! Maria! Get in here! The show's starting! Where's Dad?"

"He's out on a call, don't you remember?" Jace reminded her.

Chrystal hoped Vinnie would get back in time to see at least part of the show. Half an hour ago the telephone had rung with an emergency.

"It's a perforated fuel line, honey," he'd said apologetically on his way out. "It's that new customer with the Rolls. I don't want to let him down. I'll be back soon's I can." He'd kissed her and gone.

Chrystal sighed. Before, Vinnie had *always* been around. Now, it seemed, he was hardly ever home.

She supposed she should be grateful. But everything had happened so fast! After Vinnie had successfully repaired Milton Shrubsole's old Buick, word had spread like wildfire through the town. There was finally—at last—a good mechanic in Boonton Harbor!

Chrystal's eyes misted over. Dear, sweet Milton. He had done this for her. She was so happy he'd finally found a nice woman who loved him. . . .

On the TV screen Casey Kasem was pushing his microphone into celebrity faces. Nicholson. Fonda. Douglas.

Suddenly there was a great roar as Barron Heatter stepped out of his limo, a starlet on each arm.

"Bar-ron! Bar-ron!" could be heard above the din of the crowd. Chrystal leaned forward for a better look.

There was Rosalie, looking positively dazzling. God, she looked happy! Chrystal remembered the last time she'd seen her, a year ago, at that awful weekend at Windsor. Rosalie looked like a different person.

Casey Kasem extended the mike to the handsome, craggy-faced man with Rosalie. "And now, folks, here is the producer who made this all possible. Kermit O. Fineberg! Hi, Kermit!"

Kermit waved to the camera. "Actually, Casey, the credit should go to my beautiful wife, Rosalie. . . ."

Chrystal watched as Rosalie took the microphone. "Casey, I'd like to say a special hello to two people who should be sharing the spotlight tonight. Chrystal O'Neill Malatesta, the author of *Sweet Awakenings*. And our star, Daphne Banks Funt, who, I'm sure you know, is, at this very moment, in the hospital having a baby." Rosalie blew a kiss.

"Mom! Can you believe? She said your name!" exclaimed Heather.

Jace put his arms around her in a big hug. "Nice going, Mom," he said.

Just then the front door opened. "Hey, guys," said Vinnie. "I didn't miss the show, did I?"

He came over and stood behind the sofa, his hands on Chrystal's shoulders.

She looked up at him. He looked tired. All this was hard on him. Being the husband of a celebrity was never easy, even if the celebrity was only a writer.

It had taken Vinnie months to finally read her book.

When he'd finished, he'd seemed depressed. She tried to find out what the problem was, but Vinnie seemed reluctant to say.

At last he said, sheepishly, "Chrystal, I gotta

know. That dame in the book—the one that lets the old letch get into her pants—she ain't you, is she?"

Chrystal noticed the tiny vein pulsating in Vinnie's forehead—a sure sign of misery. She kissed him tenderly and assured him, again and again, that *Sweet Awakenings* was a work of fiction. That she'd taken certain details from her background, mixed them all up with details from a million other lives, and made it into a story.

Had she convinced him? She looked up at him now. The pride and love in his eyes were clearly meant for her.

She put her hands on his.

"You didn't miss anything," she said. "Not a blessed thing, darling."

Daphne and Sid

Daphne was grateful there was a television set in the labor room. But how was she going to watch the premiere of *Sweet Awakenings* with Sid hovering above her?

She closed her eyes and started to pant.

"Oh my God, Daphne! *Another* contraction? Where the hell is Finkelman? Just like an O.B.! Never around when you need him!"

He squeezed her hand until it was over. Finally, as the contraction ebbed, she was able to smile. "Take it easy, Sid," she said. "People have babies every day!"

"Yeah? Well *I* don't!"

A nurse passed by in the hallway. Sid darted

out and grabbed her. "Nurse! Do something! My wife is about to have a baby!"

The nurse looked at Sid. "This is the maternity floor, mister. Everyone in here is going to have a baby." And then she looked at Daphne. She looked closer and came into the room. "Aren't you . . . ?"

Daphne closed her eyes as another contraction started to build. "Yes . . ." she panted, blowing shallow little breaths. "I am."

The nurse ran from the room. On the television screen she saw Rosalie Fineberg blow a kiss to someone. Dear Rosalie! She owed her so much. For one thing, because of Rosalie, she never had to eat yogurt again. Because of Rosalie, she was now a star. Since *Sweet Awakenings* the scripts had been arriving by the bushel. She had her choice now—more than one choice. She could work whenever she wanted to, or even not work *until* she wanted to. And she wasn't so sure she wanted to work, what with the baby and all.

She was certainly a lucky woman.

Nora Haddock Bloom, on the other hand, wasn't such a lucky woman. Sid had heard through the psychiatric grapevine that Nora had lapsed into a catatonic stupor. She was in a sanitarium somewhere in Holland, where she was said to perpetually chant, "Later, Josiah! Later! You can't die yet!"

* * *

Three nurses ran into the room with autograph pads in their hands. In their midst was Harvey Finkelman, M.D., looking harried, as usual.

"It's about time!" Sid exclaimed.

Harvey gave Sid a condescending smile. "Take it easy, Sid. You look like hell."

Exasperated, Sid said, "Thanks a lot, Harvey. For godsakes, will you do something?"

Finkelman placed his hand on Daphne's hard-as-a-rock belly. "Well, well," he said softly, "what have we here?"

"Miss Banks, could we have your autograph, please?" asked the nurse.

Daphne obliged, even as Dr. Finkelman wheeled her into the delivery room.

Twelve minutes later—at the very moment *Sweet Awakenings* premiered on the silver screen—little Rose Chrystal Funt made her own debut.

Both received rave reviews.

Estrella

In the small house on Corrado Petaluma, she sat in front of the television. She didn't often watch—the programs were so silly—but tonight there was something special. A premiere from Hollywood. And her darling Bluma, the child of her brilliant José, was all excited.

"Abuelita!" Bluma cried excitedly. "Look! There! It is that nice Mrs. Fineberg, who gave me the ride from the airport last year. The ride to school!"

Estrella Carmelita Juanita DeSouza reached for her bifocals. Without them she could hardly make out the tiny, fuzzy images on the screen. Squinting, she saw an attractive rich lady with her hair all tight and pulled back like she was ashamed of it. She could never understand why some women tried to hide their hair. She, Es-

trella, had always worn her hair loose and
free. . . .

"Someday, I would like to take you to Califor-
nia, to Hollywood, Abuelita," said Bluma.
"When I finish school and become a certified
public accountant, I will have lots of money, and
then I will show you many new places."

Who needed new places? Estrella thought,
but didn't say. She had tried a new place—New
York, in fact. And what had it brought her but
pain? Of course it had brought her José, and he
was her pride and joy, but the cost was so high.
Even now, after all these years, she was still
paying for what had happened in New York.

Her darling Bluma reached over and
switched off the television. The girl was so
lovely. She was so proud of her. A college girl,
she was.

"Abuelita," Bluma said. "Do you remember
when I wrote to you last year? About the man
who died in my arms? The professor?"

Estrella's heart began to pound. She rocked
slowly back and forth in her chair. *"Sí, "* she said.

Bluma didn't say anything for a long moment.
"Well, I didn't tell you everything, Abuelita."

Estrella picked up her knitting. She tried to
keep her face expressionless. She knew what
was coming. She had dreamed about it for a
year.

"Well, the man, he was a professor. He said
something just before he died. It was a name."

Estrella's fingers flew deftly as she knit. She would not look at Bluma. She would not risk revealing the secret she had kept locked within herself for all these years. "What name was that, *mia paloma,* my precious?" she asked, controlling her voice.

"Well," said Bluma, uneasily. "It sounded like he said Estrella." Bluma paused and looked up. "He said your name, Abuelita."

So, she thought. He did love me after all. Bloom, her darling darling. She could see him so clearly, standing in the alley in his knickers. How sweet and funny he was, with his red hair and his big nose. And his big pecker. She couldn't help but smile.

"Abuelita?" Bluma asked. "Did you know him?"

Know him? She hadn't stopped thinking about him, not once, not even for a moment.

It had all happened so fast. Mama had taken one look at her rounding belly and known in an instant what had happened in the alley. That very night they had dragged her, kicking and screaming, to the airport, put her on a plane back to San Juan, and warned her not to try and see her beloved Bloom ever again.

"El es un maldito canto de sangano! Que no respeta la familia!" Papa had screamed.

And so she'd found herself back in Puerto Rico, where she'd had to bring up little José all by herself. Papa, in shame, had left Brooklyn for

Connecticut, where some of his cousins were able to get him a job cleaning in a school there.

But time heals all things. José had turned out to be a wonderful *nino,* a boy who could fix anything. He had grown up strong and smart, smarter than any of her cousins' children. He found a good job fixing televisions in the big hotels. He had married a good but delicate woman who, alas, had died giving birth to her darling Blumacita.

It had been many years, but she had never forgotten her Bloom. Under her bed, in an old crate, were hundreds of yellowed and aging clippings she'd carefully cut from newspapers and magazines. Clippings that told of the many accomplishments of her wonderful Bloom, the father of her José.

Someday, maybe, she would give those clippings to José and tell him the truth. Someday.

But not yet.

"Abuelita," Bluma said again. "Did you know him, the professor?"

Estrella smoothed Bluma's wild black hair back from her beautiful face. It was amazing how Bluma reminded her of herself, the way she used to look. She kissed Bluma on the forehead.

"Don't be silly, Blumacita," Estrella said. "How would a poor old woman like me ever know an important man like that?"

Desperately seeking Mr. Right

Personals
by Susan Lois

A wildly sexy, hilariously funny novel about a trio of gorgeous, brainy, and bored housewives who turn to the personal ads to try to make their dreams of love come true. The responses are everything they wanted—and more than they can handle.

16945-3 $3.95

Ever fantasize about having a mad, impetuous

FLING

Sensuous. Discreet. Astonishingly passionate, but with <u>no strings</u> attached? Kelly Nelson did, as she approached her 32nd birthday, so her two best friends arranged a one-night fling as a surprise present. Only problem was that Kelly, accustomed to juggling the demands of a solid marriage, two children, and a successful career, wasn't prepared for what happened next. Neither were her two best friends...her kids... her husband...or her incredibly sensitive, sensuous lover.

by PAMELA BECK and   12615-0 $3.95
PATTI MASSMAN